MONSTER

CHRISTOPHER CUNNINGHAM

This is a work of fiction. Names, characters, places, and incidents are products of the authors imagination or are used fictitiously and are not to be construed as real. Any resemblance to actual events, locales, organizations, or persons, living or dead, is entirely coincidental.

MONSTER: A Tale of Existential Horror, Copyright © 2021 by Christopher Cunningham. All rights reserved. Printed in the United States of America and/or other authorized locales. No part of this book may be used or reproduced in any manner whatsoever without written permission except in the case of brief quotations embodied in critical articles and reviews.

Cover Designed by: MiblArt

Visit my website at: strangegatherings.com

First Edition

ISBN: 9798548459206

ASIN: B09CRSNVCG

Chapter One

Brad Turner gripped the steering wheel tight. A familiar pressure clutched his chest. He knew its cause, but he'd never felt it as strong as it was now. Like a straitjacket pulled to extreme, or the constraining, neurotic squeeze of tight places. It was inescapable, but he tried his best to ignore it. This wasn't the right time. It might never be. He drew in a deep intentional breath and slowly let it drain away.

Beside him, in the passenger seat of the road-battered hatchback, sat his wife, Sarah. The truth was, she wasn't his wife. But she wasn't really his girlfriend either. Things were more complicated than that. It wasn't a question of whether he loved her, but whether he could do so forever. The commitment of marriage loomed over him like a storm cloud, an inescapable maze, a beckoning door that would lock forever behind him.

He never told Sarah how he felt, not really. The words stuck in his throat unable to overcome their own gravity. They were overblown - he knew that. And like a lot of things, holding them inside left him nauseous and prone to attacks of stress. Still, all this being true, he would marry her if he thought it would make her happy. That's what mattered, wasn't it? It was the right thing to do. There were expectations.

At twenty-four, Sarah was three years younger than Brad. She had a cute round and freckled face surrounded by mid-length mousey brown hair. She had a small frame and was extra curvy after the birth of their son. Sarah wore a long thin cross around her stippled neck. She carried it like a shield against the evils of the world. And though her energy and spontaneity could be contagious and at times uplifting, they could be equally exhausting. Even now on this unexpected road-trip, she showed a vivacity that seemed almost delusional considering the events of the day.

She was turned facing the backseat and singing that song about the bus and how its wheels turned round and round. Brad listened with tight muscles and the growing pressure inside. If the song of the sirens could drive a man to madness, then this had to be its inspiration.

Sarah sang to their one-year-old son, Jason. The rear-view mirror was turned down so that Brad could see him strapped into the child safety seat. It occurred to Brad that maybe Jason had inherited his intolerance to anxiety. The boy had been crying since they got back on the road. The high-pitched, frustrated screaming drilled into Brad's brain. Brad did everything he could to push it out of his head and suppress an urge to scream in return. He bottled it up and hoped that his son would exhaust himself and fall back to sleep. It was only a matter of time, he thought. Of course, Brad had been wrong before.

Sarah had been trying to calm the boy for the last twenty minutes. At first, she'd tried to talk him down, as if reasoning with a one-year-old made any sense at all. Failing that, she'd started to sing. Finally, Jason began to settle, and Brad was left wondering which was worse, the screaming child or the happy little sing-along.

Through the windshield he watched the thick woodland pass by as they meandered along the unfamiliar road. He'd been watching for some sign of where they might be – a road marker, or a gas station. Some time had passed since he'd seen any sign at all. He took turns shaking the tension from his stiff hands and continued his controlled breathing.

Beyond the wall of trees, the forest on either side of the road was black. It was late afternoon, and a pre-mature darkness was coming on. Huge dark clouds billowed overhead ushering more than a rumor of storm. Leaning forward to look at the sky, Brad could smell rain through the vents in the dashboard.

Ahead, a small break in the clouds was outlined with the glow of bright colors – red, orange, gold and purple. The deep opening revealed a patch of distant blue. Brad recalled seeing paintings of sunset clouds in colors like these, so vibrant that they could not possibly exist in nature. This was one of those skies. For just a moment it distracted from his discomfort. But it did not last.

Black, roiling clouds swept in and swallowed the opening as he watched, banishing it in favor of the coming night. A painful lump formed in his throat as the encroaching darkness flashed silently with electricity. An intuition of danger crossed his mind, like a whispered warning from some long dormant ancestor drowned in his genetic pool.

Then the rain began. Drops as big as golf balls struck the windshield with such force that in a moment of surprise Brad thought they might break the glass.

Sarah stopped singing and turned suddenly around. "Oh, my goodness!" she said as the windshield wipers began their losing battle. "It's pitch black out there. Do you have your lights on?"

"Yes, yes, I have the lights on," Brad grumbled. "I still can't see shit."

"Should we pull over?" she asked.

Brad shot a glance at her. "If I could see!" he snapped. He took in another long breath and slowly released it. "I don't want to run us into a ditch."

He looked down at the speedometer. He had already slowed to nearly a crawl. He reached up and readjusted the rear-view mirror. Only blackness and cascading water rushed down the back window. In a moment he brought the car to a complete stop.

Jason was screaming again. It was blood curdling, as if he were being horribly tortured in the darkness of the backseat. The sound made Brad wince.

"Where are we?" Sarah asked. "Do you know?"

"Somewhere near Petersburg, I think, or maybe its Parkersburg," he answered. "I haven't seen any signs in a while." He started to roll down his window, hoping to catch a sign of where they were, but the rain battered him and splashed in his undefended eyes. Turning away he raised the window. In an instant his left side was soaking wet. The sound of rain pounding on the roof of the car was rivaled only by the screaming from the backseat. Brad reached forward and turned on the hazard lights. The bright orange flashers were dimmed by the veil of falling water.

"What are you doing?" Sarah asked.

Brad looked over at her. She was only dimly lit by the dash lights and the pulsing hazards. Her eyes were wild and darting. He pulled back from her. It wasn't like her to be afraid of anything, least of all the weather. Her stiff body and a foreign expression made her look artificial, like a stranger. It repurposed the uneasiness Brad had been feeling in his chest.

And still the screaming went on.

"We're going to sit here and wait," he said. "Just keep an eye out around us. If someone else comes along, we don't want them to smash into us... It's just a cloud burst. It'll be over in a couple of minutes."

Sarah stared at him and then nodded her head. She sat silent now. Even the screaming of her child had no effect. Her well of positivity seemed emptied and dry. Brad watched her for a moment. He saw the glow of red dash light in her eye and washed across her face. Her subtle movements seemed oddly mechanical in the strobing orange.

Brad tried to swallow. Among all this water, his mouth was parched. He licked raindrops from his lips.

Turning back to the blackness beyond the window, a slow sensation crept over him, rising like a poor blind creature crawling from a bubbling primordial pool. It left an uneasy impression of something in the dark. The clouds high above flashed again but illuminated only rain. He felt an unexpected detachment, as if he were merely an observer watching a nightmare unfold. Then something touched his feet, a cold and wet soaking grasp.

Sarah gasped and jerked her body. She practically jumped as she raised her feet up off the car floor and pulled them beneath her. "Water!" she cried. "We're filling with water!"

"Oh shit!" Brad shouted. He put the car into gear and started to pull slowly forward. As he did the water around his feet raised almost to his knees.

"Stop!" Sarah shouted. "That's deeper!"

Brad threw the transmission into reverse and the car began to back up. The water level slowly dropped. "That's it!" he said. "That's it!"

Then it began to rise again. He stopped. "It's behind us too, I can't see shit!" he said.

He rolled down his window again. This time he gave little notice to the downpour outside. He leaned his head out the window and looked around. There was only blackness. He had never seen a darkness so complete – so unnatural. It was as if they were afloat on an immense black sea. His headlights and taillights were the only steady illumination. He saw white rain in front of them and red rain behind. In the flash of the hazard lights strobed the bombardment of raindrops stretching across the rising plane of water.

"There's nothing out here?" his words erupted loud and high. He turned to Sarah and realized that she didn't understand the bizarre reality of what he'd seen. "I mean there's literally nothing out there! There's no trees, no forest. I don't see anything!"

"Go!" Sarah shouted. "Get us out of here!"

Brad put the car back in gear and it started to reverse again. The water raised as they moved. Then the car jerked. He felt, more than heard, the engine sputter. It coughed, sick and drowning. Then it died. A gang of failure lights lit up the dash, a loud buzzer began to wail. Jason's relentless screaming stabbed like a sharp spike into the back of Brad's neck. Water was now up to his waist.

"We've got to get out of the car!" he said turning to Sarah. "We need to get on the roof!"

He looked at her in the darkness and saw her face in flashes of orange and red. It was shuddering. Her eyes were completely black, like rotted fruit. Her mouth quivered cold in uncontrolled spasms. In the strobing hazards, she seemed to sneer at him. His heart pounded like a hammer and anvil.

Brad unhooked his seatbelt and turned around. Up on his knees he reached back over his seat and unstrapped screaming Jason from his bondage. He could feel Sarah's presence beside him. For a moment he hesitated, his mind racing, then he handed his son to her.

"I'll climb through first. Hand Jason up to me and then I'll help you," he said with as much calm as he could manage.

She sat staring back at him. He could see the whites of her eyes again. She clutched Jason close as the water was almost up to window level. She was shivering.

"Are you with me, Sarah?" he shouted at her. "Can you do this?"

She seemed to snap out of it for a moment. She nodded her head abruptly. "Yes," she said. "Yes."

With his back to the window, he slipped through so that he was sitting on the door frame. He half stood and lunged with his arms to get some grip on the roof. The rain stung his back. It bounced off the roof and into his eyes. He managed to get hold of the lip where the windshield met the roof, then climbed from the open window on top of the car. He flattened his body, then spun so he could face the opening below him.

"Sarah!" he shouted. "I'm here! Hand him up!"

Just then the car shifted. Brad scrambled to regain his grip as the car jerked and spun and started to move. Barely floating, it bounced on its rubber tires making his hold more precarious. He looked about, trying to see where the flood was taking them. Blackness stretched in every direction. The clouds above flashed silently again. No thunder, no bolt of lightning. But it lit up the void.

There was a vast plane of flat sea stretching off into infinity, textured and alive with the bombardment of rain. The forest and the surrounding ridgelines were gone, vanished like ghostly vapors. In his swirling state, he questioned both his eyes and his sanity. Somehow the rain had washed away the world. But there was something more than that. It sprang from an overwhelming presence around him. As if some giant leviathan circled below the surface of the flood ready to capsize and devour them whole.

He looked down again and saw water flowing into the car through the window.

"Sarah!" he shouted. "Sarah!"

He leaned further out, tempting his fragile hold. He reached down blindly through the window but felt only water. The car was moving swiftly now, bounding within an invisible current. He held on for his life. Brad raised his head, but the pounding rain blurred and blinded. He dared not release his grip to clear his vision. Then the blackness that surrounded them flowed into his mind and left all his thoughts in darkness.

Christopher Cunningham

* * *

When Brad Turner next opened his eyes, he was lying in a strange bed. The light around him was soft and it took a moment for his vision to regain focus. The small room was clinical. This was no hospitality suite. There was a window with faded, sun-stained, yellowed curtains. The walls around him were unadorned. The bed was a hospital bed, but it was old. It had a thin mattress and chrome rails raised on each side, both rails showed signs of spotty rust. There were no push-button adjustments, only manual levers and springs. A glass I.V. bottle with clear liquid hung from a chrome stand on one side of him, its caramel-colored rubber tube draped down and inserted into his arm with an oversized metal needle. On his other side, a small nightstand supported a translucent plastic bottle that smelled of what he guessed was his own urine. All around him the walls and ceiling were in disrepair. Faded institutional green paint peeled and hung like dead garden leaves. In some places, he could see through the broken horsehair plaster to the wood lathe beneath. Everything smelled sterilized in pine soap.

He was not alone. Standing in front of the window, staring like a statue through the luminous curtains, was a woman. She was a nun. Dressed all in black, but for the white linen coif beneath her veil. She stood so still that she barely disturbed the dust suspended in the air around her.

Brad opened his mouth but found that his throat was too dry to form words. He made a scratchy guttural sound.

The nun turned and showed her face for the first time. Her features were like the room around her. Her skin was pale and paper-thin. From where Brad lay a few feet away, he could see tiny blue veins just beneath the surface. Her wrinkles were so deep and prominent that they cast shadows beyond their creases. Her face had no emotion, only a cold look of examination.

She turned without a word and glided across the floor and into an antechamber beyond his view. A light came on and he heard water begin to run. In the old woman's shadow, he saw her filling a pitcher. She returned a moment later and placed the pitcher and an empty glass on the stand beside his urine bottle, then she came closer and raised the back of his bed. Her large chest nearly brushed his unwilling face as she leaned over him. She smelled strongly of mothballs. Next, she filled the glass and handed it to him.

He drank greedily, choked as it went down the wrong way, cleared his throat, then drank again. His parched body absorbed the water like desert rain. Suddenly, memories of the flood rushed back to him. His mind filled with jumbled memories and a thousand questions.

"Where am I?" he began. "Where's my wife and my son? Are they okay?"

"Wife?" the nun asked as if the word had some meaning of which she was unaware.

"Yes, my wife. Is she here? Is my son here too? Where are they? Are they alright?"

"Someone will be with you shortly," she said. "You need to stay calm and rest."

"Rest!" Brad reacted louder than he intended. "I am resting." He closed his eyes and breathed. "Listen, I just want to know what's going on. You can understand that. Please, just tell me where I am and where my family is."

"It won't be long," she dismissed. She turned and smoothly moved across the room and passed through the door.

Brad lay with his mouth hanging open. Something was wrong. There was a reason this woman had ignored his questions. Sarah and Jason, they hadn't made it, he thought. He hadn't gotten them out of the car, and they had drowned. They'd been swept away by the flood, and they'd drowned. He'd failed, hadn't he? He'd let them die. He racked his brain trying to remember. Everything was there, right up to the moment when he was on the roof of the car, reaching inside. But everything was blank after that. It was all darkness.

An enormous sob grew within him. His eyes watered. Suddenly he threw-up. He had just enough time to lean sideways from the bed as the water in his stomach spilled onto the floor. He choked and coughed. Sticky drool hung in a long string from his mouth.

"Somebody help me!" he shouted. "Somebody fucking help!"

Brad sat up and blinked his watery eyes. A man stood in the doorway. He was a tall man, thin. He looked to be at least in his late sixties. He had short white hair peppered in black, clean shaven. He had unusual bright blue Siberian husky eyes with piercing sharp pupils. He was dressed all in black - shoes, trousers, belt and shirt – the white square of his collar set just below his Adam's apple. He looked at Brad and smiled. Stepping into the room, he stood at the foot of the bed and crossed his hands above his crotch.

"I'm Father Gabraulti," he said. "I'm the administrator here. I've been eager to talk with you, but I can see that you're a bit upset. Perhaps we should wait until you feel better. Perhaps a sedative to help you rest?"

"No, Father. No." Brad wiped the spittle from his mouth with the sleeve of his hospital gown. "I've got to know what's going on. I'll be calm. I'll be alright. I promise."

"Fine," Gabraulti said to him. "But let's take this slowly and one step at a time."

Brad took a deep breath and gradually blew it out. "Okay Father, I'm good."

"Well, I see from the identification you came in with that your name is Bradley Turner?"

"Yeah, that's right," he answered calmly. "Brad."

"Good," said Gabraulti. "Right now, you're at St. Lucius Sanitarium. You've been unconscious since shortly after arriving. Physically, you appear to be uninjured, however, it also appears that you've experienced a considerable amount of stress. We suspect that you've been involved in an accident, a traumatic event of some sort. We've been caring for you as best we can, but frankly, we've been waiting for you to wake up so that we can get to the bottom of your circumstances."

"Circumstances!" Brad stopped himself. He took a moment to control his emotion. "I'm sorry," he said. "Listen, I just want to know what happened to my family. Are they okay or not? I mean, if they're not I need to know."

"Mr. Turner," Gabraulti seemed to be choosing his words with great care. "You came to us alone, under your own power, and in a nearly catatonic state. You were unresponsive to our inquiries. By the time we began our initial examination you had fallen into a deep state of sleep. Since you've been here, the only information we've had to go on was your driver's license. Honestly, we've been hoping you would be able to answer some of *our* questions."

"I don't understand," Brad said. "I don't remember anything about coming here. There's got to be some report about what happened, right? You mean you haven't heard anything? You've got to go look. My family is out there somewhere. I just... don't remember."

"It's okay," said Gabraulti. "It'll come back to you. That's good. It will give us a place to start. Just give it some time."

"But you don't understand," Brad continued. "We don't have time. We were caught in a flood. The car got swept away and they were trapped inside. Maybe they're okay! Maybe they're out there, hurt. I don't know! They might need help!"

"Oh my," said Gabraulti. He furrowed his brow and pursed his lips. "That's terrible. Where did this happen? Do you remember where you were or where you were going?"

"We were driving. We were coming from... somewhere? I don't remember. But we were going... to...Damn it, I can't remember. But you gotta believe me. They're out there."

Gabraulti's expression turned from concern to sympathy. "I believe you," he said. "But we can't do anything until we have more information."

Brad exploded. "God damn it! You've got to start looking. I have to get out of here. It's got to be near here, right? They're out there!"

Brad ripped the covers from the bed and for the first time saw that his feet were restrained with thick leather straps. How he hadn't noticed them before seemed impossible. It was as if they had only suddenly appeared in response to his outburst. "What's going on?" he shouted.

Three black clad nuns rushed into the room. One was the old woman he'd awoken to. The others were young, their faces nondescript. The young women were suddenly on either side of him. They grabbed his shoulders and forced him back against the mattress. Next, he saw the needle. Its chamber looked as big as a test tube, the syringe, a harpoon. One of them stabbed him in the shoulder as he struggled. The women were much stronger than he expected.

"What are you doing?" he shouted. "Let me go!"

A warmth flowed from the injection site. The heat spread through his limbs as if being dipped gently into a comfortable bath. His body relaxed, and his mind followed. He was still thinking about his wife and child, wondering if they were alive or dead. And he wondered about this strange place and the restraints that kept him down. But he could no longer muster the ability to care. His world was still one of nightmare, but a smile came over his face. He closed his eyes and fell back to sleep.

Chapter Two

Whistling. It was in his dream. Brad Turner recognized the tune, but he couldn't place it. It was so familiar, but for some reason, as much as he struggled, he could not remember. It dominated his thoughts. Once again, he opened his eyes and was in the same strange room. And again, he was not alone.

Near the foot of his bed, a man was standing with his back toward him. He swiveled on his hips as he whisked a mop across the floor. He had thick jet-black hair and was dressed in dark green shirt and pants, bisected by a black leather belt. He was the source of the whistled tune. The skill with which he blew the music between his lips was astounding. The pitch was perfect. It seemed to have a chorus effect that made it sound as if two octaves were singing in harmony. Still, Brad could not place the tune. He cleared his throat.

The music stopped. The man halted his mopping and slowly turned to face Brad. The first thing that Brad noticed was the man's smile. It was warm and gentle, and it forced Brad to smile in return. The man's face was young and handsome. He was clean shaven and had thick black eyebrows and long lashes. His skin was tanned and smooth and he wore a thin white scar that ran from his chin and along his jawline back to his left ear. Although he seemed no older than his mid-thirties, his eyes had a depth of a much older man. A small white badge was sewn over his right breast pocket; it read, *M. Livengood.*

"Well, good morning Mr. Turner," he said with the friendliest tone. His spoken voice was nearly as melodic as his whistling. "How are you this morning? Feeling better, I hope."

"What time is it?" Brad asked.

The man stood leaning on his mop handle. He had no watch on his wrist and did not scan the room for a clock. "It's about quarter past ten," he answered. "I'm sorry that I woke you up. Must have been my whistling. Sometimes I don't even realize I'm doing it."

"It's okay," Brad said, still trying to shake off his sleep.

"My name's Malcolm, Malcolm Livengood. But you can just call me Mal."

"You work here?" Brad asked. "At the sanitarium?"

"That's right," he said. "I'm the custodian."

"Mal," Brad tried to sound sympathetic. "Can you help me? Can you undo my restraints?"

Livengood returned a puzzled look. "Restraints?"

"My feet," Brad said as he tugged at his sheets. He revealed his legs and saw that they were free. There were no straps there at all.

"Are you okay?" Mal asked.

"Yeah, I think so. But I've got to get out of here. Do you know where my clothes are?"

Mal lifted his mop and set it into a rolling bucket on the floor beside him. He rolled the set into the corner and leaned the mop handle against the wall. Beside the nightstand there was a narrow wooden cabinet. Mal walked over and opened the door. "Your clothes are right here," he said. "But if you came in with any personal items, then they're probably in Father Gabraulti's office. I'm sure if you ask…"

"Listen, I really need to get out of here. My wife and my kid were in an accident, and no one seems to know where they are. Are we close to anything, I mean, a town or a city?"

Mal drew his face up and rubbed the back of his neck. "You know, I'd like to help you, but this is all a bit beyond my pay grade. I'm not gonna stop you from doing what you need to do, but I think you should talk with the Father. He could probably help you better than me."

Brad lowered the chrome bars on the side of his bed then swung his feet onto the floor. It was icy cold, and he could see his reflection there. He noticed the I.V. still in his arm. He removed the tape and gently pulled the needle out. He stood up and had to grab hold of the nightstand to keep his balance. The urine bottle, now empty, almost tumbled to the floor. It had been days since he'd stood. He used his arms to guide him to the wardrobe. He found his clothes, cleaned, and folded. He used the bed to steady himself as he got dressed.

"Mr. Turner, I can see that you've got your mind made up about this," Mal began. "But I wish you'd let me get Father Gabraulti. I'd feel a lot better knowing you were healthy enough to go out on your own."

"I appreciate you not getting in my way here," Brad said to him as he stepped into his shoes. "And I'm really sorry if I'm getting you in trouble or anything. But I've got to go."

"Okay then," said Mal. "Then I'll walk you down. Least I can do, I guess."

Mal left his mop and bucket and led Brad out into the hall. Brad was still a little shaky, but he seemed to be regaining his strength. The long corridor was painted in the same institutional green, and just as in his room, the walls were in disrepair. It left Brad wondering about Mal's custodial skills. However, the green marbled asbestos floors were noticeably clean and shiny. At the far end of the hall was a wall of opaque glass block that lit the corridor as much as the fluorescent lighting overhead. The smell of sterile alcohol was strong. This place was a conundrum, it conjured images of straitjackets and shock therapy. A dull clamor of voices came from some opened doorway, though Brad couldn't make out their content or their direction. They echoed in muted mumbles.

Mal pushed through a set of swinging doors that opened to a stairwell. Brad followed him down the two flights of stairs. One of the florescent tubes above buzzed loudly and flickered overhead. Then, another set of doors opened into a wide lobby.

Brad spotted large glass doors at the far end of the open space. Bright light shined there with shades of green from the outside world. Four large, square columns held up the ceiling here. There were planters next to each; the plants within them were dead. Their spindly, twisted stalks reached upward, intertwined like long dry tentacles rising dead from the soil.

Not far from the exterior doors was a reception desk. A young nun sat there with her hands folded in front of her. She turned her head and smiled as the two men approached.

"Hello Mr. Turner. Hello Mal. Are we leaving?" she said in a calm friendly voice.

Brad stopped at the desk. It was clean and organized. There was a sign-in book opened to a blank page, no entries either in or out. A cup with a few pencils cast shadows across an old black rotary telephone. A lamp with a green glass shade. Nothing else.

"Good morning Sister Kayla," Mal said. "I'm afraid Mr. Turner here would like to be on his way. I think Father Gabraulti has his personal belongings, but I don't think he wants to wait around for them."

"I see," said the Sister. She looked up at Brad and smiled.

Her face was angelic. Brad wondered at her age. She couldn't have been more than nineteen or twenty years old. She sat very small beneath her black habit, She the picture of pale innocence.

Brad felt something when he looked at her. It was as pure as anything he'd known, like standing in the presence of a beloved sister or daughter. Of course, Brad had neither of these. But he felt an instant bond as he stood held in her gaze with no desire to be released. Feeling suddenly caught, he flushed red faced and averted his eyes looking down at the desktop.

"Are we in walking distance to a town? Is there a local sheriff or a police station nearby? I need to get in touch with someone about an accident, or missing person's or something like that."

Sister Kayla smiled at him. "I'm afraid we're quite isolated here. I'm not sure you'd want to walk that far. The nearest police station is in ………….. and that's pretty far away."

Brad stood there puzzled. Sister Kayla said the name of a town. It was the town where the nearest police station was. He heard her say it, as plain as day. He knew exactly what she was saying, but somehow, between the word leaving her lips and its meaning coalescing in his brain, it was forgotten. "I'm sorry, could you repeat that?" he asked.

"The ………….. police department is the closest, but it would be a very long walk from here. The road is long, and the forest is thick. I'm afraid you might get lost. Especially if you were caught out after dark."

"She's right about that," Mal confirmed.

Brad squeezed his temples with his hand. Once again, he could not recall the name she had just repeated for him. It was not that she had spoken gibberish. He was sure he'd heard it clearly. But it escaped him. The word floated at the edge of his mind, dangled from the tip of his tongue. He could not clear whatever blockage kept it from his reach.

"Can you call me a cab or an Uber or something?" he asked. "No wait," he stopped, patting at his empty pockets. "I don't have my wallet, no money." He looked back at her. "How about the police? Can you call the police, have them come here? I can make a report and have them give me a ride."

"I'm sorry Mr. Turner," Sister Kayla answered. "But we don't have an outside line."

"You don't have an outside line? What do you mean, you don't have an outside line?" He reached down and snatched the receiver from the phone cradle and put it to his ear.

"Mr. Turner, please!" Kayla said in reaction.

There was no dial tone, at least not one that he recognized. There was a faint humming, more like an echo reverberating from the depths of a dark damp bottomless well. Something like a voice lay buried within, a faint whisper he could not decipher. A woman's voice…was it Sarah? Was it the voice of his wife?

"Mr. Turner," a strong voice caught his attention, but it did not come from the phone.

It was Father Gabraulti walking toward him across the lobby. The old priest walked with the step of a man much younger than he appeared. He was tall and graceful in his movement. He carried a sense of confidence that made Brad stand at attention and lower the phone receiver from his ear.

"I'm so glad to see you up and about," the priest said smiling.

"What's going on here?" Brad asked shaking the phone receiver. His face felt hot. "You can't make me stay here. You've got no right!"

Gabraulti furrowed his brow. "No, of course not," he said. "You're free to go wherever you like. The choice is yours. No one is keeping you here, I assure you."

"But I don't know where I am, and the phone doesn't work. I don't know what to do!"

"Mr. Turner, please just take a moment." Gabraulti stood with an empathic grin. "I'm sure this all seems strange to you. This sanitarium is very old. It was intentionally built here in the middle of nowhere. The isolation is meant to be peaceful for our residents. But this is also why you coming here is such a mystery. It really is just as puzzling to us as it is, I'm sure, to you. But you must believe me when I say you are not a prisoner here. You are free to leave at any time."

Brad looked over his shoulder at the exterior glass doors. The sun shined brightly just beyond.

"That's right," Gabraulti continued. "The doors are right there. They're not locked. You can leave right now if you wish. I do warn you though, that we are far from the nearest community. It's quite a long walk."

"What about the phone?" Brad asked now lowering the receiver in his hand.

"The storm. Quite possibly the same storm that you described. The lines have been down ever since, and unfortunately, the phone company has never made us a priority. As you see, our system is antiquated, and believe it or not, we have no cell service here."

"Okay. Alright," Brad said, now grasping at straws. "So, you say I can leave, but it's too far to walk. I don't have a car, but I can't call for a ride. How the hell am I supposed to get away from here if I'm so free to go? Tell me that."

"Well, I am afraid that our small staff stay on at all hours. We all live here in the dormitory wing. We find that we have very little need to leave the facility. We do have a need however, to resupply. A delivery truck arrives twice a month with food and other items of need. I'm quite sure you'll be able to arrange a ride into town at the very least. From there, you can make any arrangements you'd care to. That is, unless you'd like to take your chances on the road." Gabraulti motioned toward the doors with a wave of his arm. "Circumstances may have guided you to us, but the choice is yours."

There was silence now. Brad looked about at the others. Mal stood watching him. Sister Kayla looked up at him from her desk. Gabraulti's neon blue eyes stared icy cold above his curious smile. Their waiting anticipation stretched tight as a bowstring.

"Fine," Brad finally relented.

The others released the tension of the room in a single exhale. They all seemed suddenly animated and relaxed.

"So, when is the next delivery? When does this truck come?" Brad asked.

"Mal?" Gabraulti redirected the question.

Mal raised his head. "Oh, ah… I'll have to check the schedule. Next couple of days I suppose."

"Excellent, I thought it might be sooner than later," Gabraulti said. "Now that that's settled, why don't I give you a tour. Seeing that you'll be with us for a few days. How are you feeling? Are you feeling up for a walkabout?"

"Yeah, I'm okay. I guess I don't have anything else to do but wait. But that doesn't mean I'm not crazy worried about my family. I'm not making you any promises about staying."

"I understand," said Gabraulti. "In the meantime, why don't you come with me. Let me show you around."

Mal and Sister Kayla, both gave him a friendly smile as he turned toward the priest. Brad nodded to them and gave an uneasy smile in return.

Brad and Gabraulti left the lobby and began down a wide-open corridor. It was a dim passage with many doors on either side. Exposed lighting tubes hung from the ceiling, many of them were burnt out, some flickered and buzzed. All the walls were in uniformly bad shape just as they had been upstairs. Above him he noticed that many tiles from the drop ceiling were missing and through their dark openings he saw ancient wiring and damp lead pipes. It was the floor that most caught his attention. It was in perfect repair, green marbled linoleum so shiny that he could look down and see their reflections mirrored there. Their reflections were like doppelgangers walking upside down beneath their feet.

"I'm afraid St. Lucius is not what it once was," the old priest said. "We are completely at the mercy of church funding, and it is barely enough to keep things going. This was once one of the premiere private psychiatric facilities in the state. But over time it's become less and less of a medical facility. Now it is merely a repository for lost souls."

Brad looked up at him as they walked. "I'm not sure I get your meaning."

"We have few full-time residents here. Each has a history with the church. Some are former clergy, others were parishioners, some former employees. They've each been diagnosed with rare psychological disorders. At one time or another they've been treated by some of the finest minds in their fields. Unfortunately, each one of them has run the course of their treatments. They have been unresponsive to therapies and pharmaceuticals. In the end, they've become victims of both their disease and of the healthcare system. Bankrupted and abandoned, some were left homeless on the streets. This is their home now. We hold out no promises of a cure for these people, but we have not forsaken them. We care for them and give such support as we can."

"Okay, so, madhouse for the incurably insane. Is that what you're saying? Is that where I've wound up?"

"That's not a very charitable description, Mr. Turner. I'd appreciate it if you wouldn't characterize it that way. You've been watching too much television, I imagine." Gabraulti scolded him without anger or judgment. "You'll find that we live a very calm and compassionate existence here. Most of our residents are completely peaceful. This is a society like any other. We have learned to live together and accept our place in God's plan."

"Sorry," Brad apologized. "It's just that I've been feeling a little crazy myself. I wonder if I hit my head or something. There's a lot I don't remember, and I'm really worried about my family."

Gabraulti stopped in mid-stride at an intersection in the hallway. "We didn't see any evidence of head trauma upon your examination. But it does concern me that you'd say that. Perhaps we should have a closer look. I'll talk with Sister Monica about the three of us getting together this afternoon. You remember Sister Monica. She was with you when you first woke up. She's our head nurse here."

"Sure, the creepy old nun. I remember her," Brad said.

"You really do speak your mind, don't you Mr. Turner?"

"Yeah, sorry," he answered. "My wife, Sarah, she gives me a hard time about it too."

Gabraulti smiled and nodded his head.

As they stood, stopped in the intersection, Brad noticed a set of doors in a dark alcove across from him. The doors were metal, and their bottom halves were blackened as if by fire.

"What's through there?" Brad asked.

The old priest didn't turn to look. "That's the province of Mr. Livengood. It leads to the basement. He has his quarters down there among the boilers and generators. Wisely, he keeps it locked. It's a maze down there, not really safe for anyone to be wandering around. As I said, this building is very old."

Brad nodded.

"But let me show you something that you might enjoy." Gabraulti waved his arm in the direction opposite the basement doors.

Brad followed Gabraulti's motion.

The two men walked down the short hall opposite the alcove and came to a set of opaque glass doors. Brad could smell chlorine even before Gabraulti opened the door for him.

"This is our therapy pool," the priest said.

The large, high-ceiling room was shiny and humid. The ceiling above was paneled glass and let in abundant sunlight. It made the room steamy and tropical. The swimming pool was large, perhaps forty feet long and twenty wide. The walls, columns and floor were covered with smooth beige ceramic tile. Everything looked slippery. Chrome railings led down steps into the shallow end of the bright blue water. Chrome ladders curved up from the depths of the far end. The back wall of the room was also glass paneled and Brad could see a garden of hedges and shrubs outside. Gabraulti led him along the length of the pool.

"Mr. Livengood keeps the pool immaculate, as you can see. Though it doesn't get as much use as it probably should." The pool room was an echo chamber. Gabraulti's voice and the sound of their feet against the tile reverberated.

"From time to time we chaperone resident groups for swim activities. But as a staff, we rarely if ever use it ourselves. I can't imagine Sister Monica in a swimsuit." Gabraulti winked at Brad with a smile. "But of course, you are welcome to use it at your leisure."

Brad glanced down into the cool depths. The distinctive smell was nostalgic and tempting. Perhaps later, he thought.

It was then he noticed something odd. At first his vision seemed blurred, but as he slowed his pace it grew in clarity. There was something taking shape at the bottom of the pool, something large. He came to a complete stop and gasped. It was a car. More than that, it was his car. It sat submerged in the deep water. Rippling waves of sunlight danced across the roof and hood. Brad grasped his face and leaned closer. He focused on the driver's window opening. The window was down, just as he had left it, but the interior was lost in the deep dark blue of abysmal night.

Brad's hands began to shake. Trembling ran rampant through his body. That horrible pressure returned to his chest, the same constriction he'd felt on the night of the disastrous flood. The room around him darkened, black to the horizon, and rain began to pound the water's surface. Brad was floating now, hanging above the waters. He struggled reaching for the vehicle, but he was too high, the car too deep. The pool had become a vast lake with black shores on a distant horizon. But he was not alone.

Somewhere beyond sight roamed the Leviathan. It swam huge and powerful in its ultimate maliciousness. Somehow Brad knew that it was not aware of him yet. Perhaps it did not care. But once it came upon him its indifference would surely be his destruction. As if standing with his back to a dark basement, he could feel its emanations, they seeped from its enormous pores like acidic sweat. He dared not turn and look. Somehow, doing so would expose him and draw the target of its attention. Like a child in that dark basement, he wanted to run, to escape. But floating now above the stormy waters he had no choice. He was frozen and at its mercy.

Instead, he focused on the car below him and the dark window, his wife, his son. Then he saw the pale movement. The ovoid face shifting into view. It was Sarah gazing up at him, her wide eyes caught him in their curious glare, her hair swam about her face like the mindful appendages of an octopus clung to the back of her head. Then he saw Jason, his round face just below his mother's. Brad moaned with torment. He tried to reach out but could not.

Jason looked up at his father, his emotionless eyes hammered an iron stare. Then he opened his mouth and released a horrific shriek. Bubbles of screaming breath shot from his throat in an eruption that instantly corrupted his image and that of his mother. Brad wanted to save him, wanted to save them both. He held in his own scream and hardened his will. He tried to dive into the water, but something held him back.

"Mr. Turner!" Gabraulti asserted loudly. He had Brad by his arm and opposite shoulder. Gabraulti was strong for his age. He yanked Brad back from the edge where he was leaning, almost falling into the pool.

Brad was sucked back into the moment. He stood on the edge of the pool with the old priest holding him firmly from behind. The room was silent except for his hyperventilated breathing. The sun shined down through the glass ceiling and the calm blue chlorine rich water rested motionless before him. Brad blinked his eyes vigorously, testing whether one reality might replace another. But nothing changed.

"Mr. Turner are you alright?" Gabraulti asked concerned.

Brad took a moment to regain composure. His mind was spinning. It wasn't real, he decided. It was some phantom fantasy escaping his guilt-ridden subconscious. But his armchair self-diagnosis did not comfort him. This vision, this full-blown hallucination could mean only one thing. There was something terribly wrong with him.

"I don't think so," he answered.

"I think we should cut our tour short," said the priest. "Perhaps you weren't quite ready to be up and about. Let's get you back to your room and let you rest."

"Yeah, that sounds good," said Brad. "I need to lay down. And maybe, maybe I should see that creepy old nurse. I'm not sure I'm feeling so good."

"Of course," said Gabraulti turning him gently from the pool's edge. "Let's get you back to your room.

Chapter Three

Brad sat with his feet dangling from the edge of his bed. Sister Monica held his wrist with one hand, checking his pulse. With her other hand she released air from the blood pressure cuff around his upper arm. She stood with her body almost touching him. He examined the thin skin of her face. The tiny blue veins looked like an intricate river system as seen from low orbit. The smell of mothballs wafting from her proximity made his eyes water. He wondered how she could stand it. He wondered whether she even noticed it at all.

The uncomfortable invasion of his space was only a momentary distraction from what was foremost in his mind. After the horrific vision of seeing his family in the pool, seeing them drown in their car, he was more frightened than ever. He was trying hard to believe that they were alright, that they had somehow survived the deluge. It reminded him of how important they were, even though taking on the responsibility of a family had been so hard. It was still a struggle. He remembered the uneasiness and the lack of control he'd felt before Jason was born. He remembered how Sarah had tried to make it seem alright.

"Why are you so angry?" Sarah had asked him with a scolding look on her face.

Brad looked back, frustrated. "I'm not angry...It's just...", he couldn't complete the thought. He couldn't complete the thought because he knew it was true. He was angry. He had been for a long time.

He and Sarah had this argument more than once. It became more frequent now that the baby was on the way. Brad hated to argue; he preferred to let his frustrations fester inside. He figured that one day it would lead to a coronary and a triple by-pass, but that was the wonder of the future, it always seemed so far away. At that moment he sat at their kitchen table, staring into his cup of lukewarm coffee, hoping the subject would drop. He knew better. Sarah stood across from him resting the small of her back against the edge of the counter. A crescent of her round pregnant belly hung exposed from beneath her maternity blouse. It wouldn't be long now, he thought. Jason, the name they had picked for the baby, would start pushing himself out any day now.

Brad thought things were difficult now, but when the baby came, everything would change. He only wished he'd had some say in it all. At first, he had made subtle suggestions that maybe they shouldn't keep the baby, that maybe they were too young, that they weren't ready. After all, they weren't even married. Sarah gasped. Abortion was a horrible sin, she'd said. It was murder. Once Sarah made it clear that she was going to see this through, he'd even suggested that they finally get married. But she refused. She didn't want the baby to be the reason for them to marry. If they were going to do it, she wanted it to be because they both wanted it, independent of them becoming parents. Brad struggled with the strange irony, since he didn't really want to be a parent either. He was damned either way, but he couldn't tell her that.

"What? It's just what?" she continued to press.

He closed his eyes. A physical pressure in his throat held back what was on his mind. He didn't want to lie to her; things were bad enough. Sarah was such a sweet person, so filled with positivity. She acted as if her affirmative outlook could carry the weight of the world. She believed so strongly in a higher power that would always make everything turn out right. But it made her a bit of a narcissist. Brad doubted if she was capable of understanding that misery and regret were naturally occurring qualities of human experience. He was not jealous of her attitude, but sometimes he was resentful and that also fed into his notions of guilt and inadequacy. He switched tracks and found a truth that was not as likely to upset her.

"I'm just feeling kind of lost, that's all." Ambiguity was his favored response.

"How can you say that?" Sarah changed her tone. "Everything is going so well. The baby is coming soon, we have the playpen and the crib already set up. My parents are coming to help out. Things couldn't be better."

The genuine smile she wore told him that she really meant what she was saying.

He looked up and smiled back at her. "You're right. I suppose I'm just getting anxious. Everything is going to work out, right?"

Sarah moved and stood beside him where he sat. She gently took his head and pulled him toward her so that his cheek rested against her warm belly.

"It's going to be perfect," she said. "Everything is going to be perfect."

Looking back on that now, he wasn't sure if perfect was the right word.

The old nun turned to Father Gabraulti. "Pressure is slightly elevated; pulse is 90 bpm."

"That's understandable," Gabraulti responded.

"Otherwise, he seems in perfect health," she finished. She spoke as if Brad was not even in the room with them.

"Thank you, Sister Monica," Gabraulti said.

Taking that as a dismissal, she nodded and left the room. Brad could not see her feet below her long black robes, but she seemed to roll across the floor as if standing on a wheeled platform. It was unnatural and left him with an odd curiosity. Perhaps she had no legs. Maybe she was an amputee and was using some mechanical device to move around. He tried for a moment to imagine what kind of device it might be and how it would attach to her lower body. His stomach churned as he pondered what was under the dress of the old woman.

"Well, Mr. Turner, I'm no medical doctor, but under the circumstances I'd have to say that your symptoms are stress related. I hesitate to jump to a more serious diagnosis without a more thorough examination. For now, I'd suggest simply getting more rest. If you like, I can have one of the sisters bring you something, a valium perhaps. Something to help you relax?"

"No thank you," Brad answered. "I'll be fine. I'll just lay here, maybe take a nap."

Gabraulti smiled. "Very well. I'll see that someone stops by to check on you from time to time in case you need anything."

"Thank you, Father," Brad said.

Gabraulti left the room.

Brad scanned the walls around him. The patches of exposed lathwork looked back at him. The thin black gaps between the strips of wood were like a hunter's blind, hiding watchful eyes and predators. He stood up and walked to the window, pushing aside the time-stained gossamer curtains that hung there. This was his first mindful view of the world that surrounded this strange place.

The first thing that he noticed was the forest. It was vast, stretching toward the far horizon. It was so uniform in height that it meshed into a flat plain of treetops. There were no hills or valleys or contours. From his second story vantage point he could imagine standing in a boat floating on that calm sea of forest canopy. This was not the typical Appalachian skyline he expected.

Below and to the right, there was a wide gravel area. He guessed it was outside the main entrance to the sanitarium. A gravel road extended from it and disappeared into the trees. There were no cars in the lot, nor were there tracks or depressions in the gravel giving evidence of any vehicles' passing.

The building had a wide perimeter between itself and the forest. The space appeared to be perfectly circular. On either side of the manicured lawn, stretched thick and intricate shrub gardens and flagstone paths. He could see the shapes of gray statues and fountains among the twisting labyrinths. The kept gardens were a stark contrast to the near dilapidated conditions within the building. The image gave some insight into the priorities of Mr. Livengood. Clearly, he was a groundskeeper before a custodian. Brad smiled and shook his head at the thought.

But there was something else nagging him as he stood in that room, a strange familiarity. Brad remembered visiting with his grandmother in a place like this. Grandma had lived with him and his family for as long as he could recall. She was a sweet, plump, gnome of a woman. The kind that would strike up conversations with perfect strangers in the grocery store as if they'd known each other for years, asking about their lives and giving details about her own. But as Brad grew and matured, he realized that Grandma was not the picture of mental health. What started as playful fantasies about cute little guardian angels, turned into disturbing thoughts of demonic paranoia. Grandma wound up in a place just like this. It came as no comfort for Brad to realize that anyone could lose their mind, and worse yet, that mental illness ran in families like pre-mature baldness, diabetes, and cancer.

He twitched at the sound of deep echoing laughter. It was distant, coming from behind him and down the hall. Brad turned from the window and stepped over to the open door. The hallway was empty. The high gloss floor reflected light from the ceiling. The laughter had faded, but he could hear a voice. He couldn't make out what it was saying, but there was something about its tone that made it seem more social than clinical. The last thing he wanted to do was walk in on Sister Monica and a group of her subservient nuns. What did nuns talk about, anyway, he thought? No, this was a boisterous, masculine voice. A loud conversation. He stepped out into the hall to follow the sound.

Monster

Just down the corridor, a door stood open to a large room that he recognized as a lounge. It was a bright room with many opaque windows along the far wall. Painted in the same institutional green, it was better kept than other rooms he'd seen. The shiny floor made the area seem much larger in dimension. Movement within was mirrored there in blurred and hazy images of light. Tables and chairs sat like islands about the place - they were inhabited islands.

A dozen or more people sat at tables, either alone or in small groups. Some stood near the windows gazing into the hazy light. A few sat or lay directly on the floor. One man sat at a table talking briskly to his companions. He used his arms and hands as well as his voice. Animated, he threw his head back and laughed loudly from his belly. His table mates sat swaying with hanging drool and glassy stares. But this was no doubt the laughter Brad had heard from his room.

Like taking a wrong turn in trespass of another man's property, Brad wanted to back out before anyone noticed him, but it was too late. At a small round table nearest the door a man sat alone. He was looking up at Brad. The man wore a flannel shirt open with a t-shirt beneath. He had black sweatpants and white canvas sneakers. His appearance gave the impression of relative normalcy, his brown eyes the focus of sane intelligence. With his curious expression he subtly gestured for Brad to approach.

Brad still had a strong desire to back out of the doorway and escape to his room, but the social grace of the moment forced his compliance. He stepped in and over to the table.

"Hi, you're the new guy, right?" the man said more than asked. "I'm Antony, Antony Sharpe." He reached his hand out.

Brad took his hand and shook it. "Brad Turner," he said.

"Good to meet you, Brad. Here, have a seat." He pushed one of the chairs out with his foot.

"Thanks," said Brad. "But I was just going to head back to my room."

"Oh, come on," Antony said. "Just a few minutes. Being with all these nut-bags, I'm dying for some real company."

Brad grinned and fidgeted. He was the new guy, and he didn't want to come across as a dick. It reminded him of the first day at summer camp as a kid. Surrounded by new people and not knowing who to hook-up with, hesitant to befriend the first kid to approach him. Reluctant to be an outcast, but afraid to expose himself to someone new. But this was not summer camp. He would only be stuck here for a day or two. Soon none of this would matter. Brad did his best to suppress his hesitance and apprehension. There were other things to worry about, and all he wanted was for this strange pit-stop to be over and to find out what had become of his family.

Now the discomfort of his pause was obvious. Only a few seconds, but it seemed so long. The social awkwardness forced his hand.

"Sure, I can stay for a few minutes." Brad pulled out the chair and sat down.

Antony leaned forward on his elbows. "You don't know how good it is to hang with someone normal for a change. This place - if you ain't crazy comin' in, you'll be crazy goin' out."

"I'm not sure I like the sound of that," Brad said honestly.

"Oh, I'm just fuckin' around. I been here a long time and I manage to keep it together. It's not so bad. But it's nice to have some new company, that's all I'm sayin',"

Brad smiled politely. Antony was an olive-skinned man with dark hair and sharp features. He was older than Brad, maybe in his mid to late thirties. Brad guessed that he was Italian or Greek, something Mediterranean. He based that on nothing more than his appearance and he scolded himself for that. Sure, it was a stereotype, but stereotypes didn't exist in a vacuum. Brad felt stereotyped himself sometimes. People assumed he was a normal family guy. A well-balanced husband and father, hardworking and striving to provide for his family. Those assumptions made him feel like an imposter. He felt anything but normal.

"So, you had some kind of accident, huh?" Antony began.

Brad stiffened and raised his eyebrows.

"Yeah, word gets around pretty quick round here," Antony said.

"There was a flash flood," Brad answered him. "Our car got washed off the road. I was with my family, and I don't know what happened to them. I'm just waiting to get out of here, so I can find them."

"Yeah, family... that's tough," Antony was smiling and nodding his head. "That's why I'm here. I had a death in my family, and I've had a bad time dealing with it. Couldn't work no more. Do the things I used to do. It's fucked up, I know."

"You don't understand," Brad leapt in. "My family's missing. For all I know, they're out there looking for me. There's this missing time, right after the accident. Then I wound up here. I don't know. That's why I've got to get out of here. They say I can leave anytime I want, but I don't even know where we are. They say there's a delivery truck coming, in a few days. I can hitch a ride."

"Yeah," Antony looked about the room. "Yeah, everybody's got a story. Some kinda tragedy."

"It's not just a story!"

"Yeah, everybody's got a story, alright." Antony pointed across the room. "See that lady over there?"

Brad followed his finger to where the loud man was still talking at his table mates. There was one woman there. She was the only one in attendance without a string of drool shimmering in the window light. Middle-length graying hair topped her middle-aged body. She wore a simple blouse and pants, flat shoes. A small silver cross hung around her neck and rested on ample breasts; cheap gaudy rings adorned her fingers. She wasn't terribly heavy, but with her chin resting on her chest she had a double neck supporting her face. If she wasn't asleep, she was clearly nodding through the loud man's monologue.

"That's Edith," said Antony. "She's our mystery lady. Saw something terrible, they say. But you wouldn't know it from her. She won't talk about it. If you try, you'll see why. Sometimes she'll just walk away. Sometimes you'll just get the look… or the catatonia. I don't know what it is she saw, but it sure musta been awful. Drove her right outta her mind. Course other times, if you catch one of her moods, she'll whack out and get all manic and crazy. She's like that damned box of chocolates, you know?" He smiled as if pleased by his use of the metaphor.

"And that guy, the one that's runnin' his mouth, that's Ray. Don't get caught in a conversation with him. He's another one you don't want to catch at the wrong time. Used to be a priest, big deal outside of Chicago somewhere. But God got in his head, see. Started thinking he was some kinda new messiah or some shit like that. One of those snake handling nuts. Had a tight group of followers, ready to follow his ass straight up to heaven. Turns out they had it backwards. He murdered the whole bunch. Mixed up some kinda kool-aid with frog toxin."

Brad's stomach turned. He watched the man from a distance. He hadn't stopped talking since before Brad arrived and he showed no sign of slowing down. He was a big, heavy-set man in his mid to late fifties, easily two-hundred-seventy-five pounds. He wore his brown hair long down his spine and tied in the back. He was the best dressed person in the room, in khaki's, oxford shirt and shiny polished brown leather shoes and belt. A long black coat hung from the back of his chair and trailed on the floor. He slapped the table with his big hands as he spoke. For the first time Brad tried to parse what he was saying. He seemed to be proselytizing about something, but in the end, Brad couldn't follow his point. It seemed nothing more than a word salad. Brad had a horrible image of him standing in self-actualized victory over a congregation of foaming mouthed corpses.

"And then there's Mary," Antony continued. Now he was pointing toward a young woman sitting cross-legged in the far corner of the room.

She was about Brad's age, certainly less than thirty. She had long dirty-blonde hair that hung around her pretty face. Her body was thin. She wore a tight-fitting shirt that showed off her attractive form. Tight blue jeans covered her legs, and her feet were bare. She sat staring at her hands, held palms up in her lap. She seemed to be playing some kind of game with her fingers. Brad couldn't help noticing pert nipples beneath the fabric of her shirt.

"You're a married man. You need to stay clear of that one. She's one of those *sex addicts*, if you know what I mean. She'll jump from one person to the next like a flea, without even cleaning up. And it don't matter... man, woman, priest, nun. She'll try to hump you in your sleep if you're not careful. Had a husband from a rich family, contributed a lot a money to the church, I hear. Poor dumb bastard didn't find out til too late that she'd been screwin' half the state. Finally caught her doin' a roomful of teenaged boys."

"Holy crap," Brad said. He found it hard not to stare at her.

"You got that right," said Antony. "Cost a bundle to keep that outta the papers. And the church did their part too. She's here and she ain't goin' nowhere."

Brad turned back to Antony. "No wonder you've been starved for company," he said. "This is quite a bunch." He leaned closer and lowered his voice. "What about the others in here? What else do you have?"

"Oh, the rest of these nut-bags are just a bunch of idiots. They're all just whacked out of their minds. Harmless for the most part." He paused. "Now the real psychos, they're supposedly locked up over in the West Wing. They don't let us over there, and they sure as shit don't let them out. And it's a good thing too. Those fuckers will kill ya. That's what I heard."

A change came over the room. It was quiet now. Brad looked away from Antony and was immediately caught in the gaze of the loud ex-priest, Ray. The big man had stopped talking and was now half turned in his chair and staring at Brad. His brow was furrowed and his body language tense and focused.

"Oh shit," Antony said under his breath. "Don't look him in the eyes, it'll just set him off. It's like starin' down a grizzly bear."

Brad did as he was told. He looked down at the floor and turned slightly away. But he saw the hulking shape of Ray in the shiny floor. The big man stood slowly up from his seat.

"You," came Ray's boisterous voice.

Brad couldn't tell whether that was a pronouncement or a question. He shifted his view to look at him, but still avoided eye contact.

"You're the new guy," Ray said with clenched fists. "We've been expecting you. We've all been expecting you." As he turned his large body, he sent his chair sliding away behind him.

Brad was back in summer camp facing down the bully. The truth was, Brad had never gone to summer camp, but he'd seen enough movies to be familiar with the tropes. His own muscles tensed, blood pressure rising. An acidic taste seeped from his glands and burned his mouth. Brad pushed himself and his chair back from the table.

Ray took a heavy step toward him.

Suddenly another voice.

"Good afternoon, folks." Mal Livengood was standing in the doorway leaning on his mop handle. "I hate to interrupt, but lounge time is over. I've got to get to these floors, you know."

Brad watched as Ray lowered his head and averted his eyes from Livengood. The mood of the room changed in an instant. Ray seemed subdued by Mal's arrival, intimidated maybe.

"Come on now, everyone back to your rooms," Mal smiled.

Everyone stood up now. No one made a fuss. They began to move and shuffle in line toward and then through the door. Even Antony said nothing as he joined the queue. Brad waited until last before he stepped toward the door. Mal held up a finger, halting him until everyone had passed and moved on down the hall.

"So, how are you, Mr. Turner?" he asked. "I understand you had an *incident* earlier?"

"Yeah," Brad answered. "An incident."

"I stopped by your room to say hello and you weren't there," Mal said. "I guessed that you came down here. I hope there's nothing amiss."

"Well, unless you count that giant psycho who looked like he was going to "fee, fie, foe" my ass. Well, then everything is just fine," Brad answered.

Mal smiled and nodded. "Oh, I don't think you have to worry about Mr. Ray. He's big and daunting, no doubt, but he's just a talker. I can't recall him ever hurting anyone. Not since he's been here."

"I guess murdering a bunch of people is not a problem, huh?" Brad said in return, his tension just now beginning to fade.

"You've been talking to Antony?"

"Yeah," he said. "He seems like the only normal person in here."

"Did he tell you why he's here?" Mal asked.

"Yeah. Some coping problem. He said there was a death in his family and that he's had a hard time dealing with it. I know it's different from my situation, but I'm beginning to understand how that must feel."

"But did he tell you the circumstances?"

"No, not really."

"Listen," Mal began. "I just work here. It's not my place to talk about people and what they do. But you need to understand that in this place, things aren't always what they seem. Not everything you hear is the truth. Sometimes it's impossible to tell the difference. The death in Antony Sharpe's family was his ten-year old son. Antony Sharpe took a knife and cut out the boys' heart. He murdered his own son.

Chapter Four

Brad found a tray of food waiting for him when he returned to his room. Hunger was the furthest thing from his mind, but after picking at it for some time he managed to clean his plate.

He stepped into the bathroom and stood in front of the sink. The small room had a pedestal basin, a toilet and a tiled shower stall with a brown-stained plastic curtain pulled back. A chrome rod supported a single bath towel. The square wall tiles were faded pink in color; the grout between them was old and gray, some was missing. The tiles themselves were in the same disrepair. Many pieces were broken, cracked or no longer in place, leaving patches of rough mortar beneath.

In front of him hung a medicine cabinet with a mirrored door. Inside he found it was shallow with narrow shelves. They were mostly empty. A paperclip, a rusty razor blade, and a worn and faded penny sat as a set abandoned. Brad closed the cabinet door and looked at himself in the mirror. The old glass was surrounded by a band of chrome plated metal. Much of the chrome was chipped off unmasking the dull gray material beneath. His reflection was blurred and slightly warped, but even so, he could see the dark depressions around his eyes, his disheveled hair, and his razor stubble. He looked like shit, he thought. He felt like shit too.

Back into the room he saw through the window that it was dark outside. It was later than he expected. He didn't remember the sunset or dusk. As far as he knew, it had been fully light just a few minutes before. Surely, his attention had been elsewhere. He shook off the confusion and stepped up to the window.

A sliver of moon must have been somewhere above and out of his sight. It cast just enough light that he could make out the sea of treetops that stretched out to the horizon. It was a vast dark mass like the tops of silent storm clouds. Below, spotlights from the building lit up the gravel lot. It was empty. Then something else caught his eye, a sign of movement in the gardens below.

Among the shrubs and hedges and twisting paths, he saw shapes slinking about. There were many. His first impression was one from his childhood. He was reminded of cave crickets. He'd seen these awful insects creeping about in basements and dark places; their long thin appendages casting unnatural shadows and confusing their shape and size. They moved with a slow mindless gait yet were capable of explosive leaps and speed enough to startle the most ready observer. The memory of their alien appearance made Brad cringe.

He dismissed the impression. Whatever was in the garden below was big, much bigger than tiny cave crickets. Still, it was impossible for Brad to tell the true scale of these things among the contrast of light and deep shadow. They might have been people, he thought, residents of the facility out after dark, but for the bizarre way they crept about like mindless crustaceans roaming a dark ocean reef. One of them was slowly inching toward an area of light. Brad watched, waiting. Suddenly it stopped frozen in place.

Brad knew why. Something had changed. A feeling more than a physical sign.

Whatever they were that roamed the garden, they reacted together in mass. Like the cave crickets of his memory, they sprang in a direction away from his view. Brad leaned into the glass to see better. Some of these things leaped as high as the hedges before they disappeared out of his sight. Still, he could not get a clear image of them. He had the new impression of a herd of deer scrambling at the coming of a predator. This explanation made more sense regarding their reaction, but it did not convince him. He did, however, share in the sensation he was witnessing, and that of the all too familiar pressure and anxiety gripping his chest.

Now he recognized the source. It was the Leviathan. It had returned. Vast and uncaring it swam across the unseen void in his imagination. Brad could picture it roaming just below the surface of the forest canopy, feeding on the plankton and krill of its own desires. It embodied a power so great its mere whim could destroy worlds. It was a giant and Brad just a skin mite clinging undetected in an eyelash, awaiting a teardrop deluge to wash him away. He could not see it with his eyes, but he knew it was close, somewhere in a physical realm so near he could almost touch it. A realm where he teetered on the edge of falling and becoming part of some nightmare reality. A place where all hope of finding his family would be lost forever.

Monster

Now suddenly exposed, he wrenched himself from the window and pressed his back tightly against the wall of his room.

There was a dark silhouette standing in his doorway.

"I'm sorry to have startled you," came Sister Monica's monotone voice. She slid into the light, and he could see her textured face. Her eyes caught him in their grip, but she seemed not to notice the shock that must have been painted all over him.

Brad spun back in front of the window. Outside there was only darkness. The omnipresence of the Leviathan was gone even as he searched the garden below and saw nothing.

"I must be losing my mind," he said to himself.

"I've been asked to include you in this evening's group session," Sister Monica said.

"What?" Brad slowly spun from the window. "Group session? I'm not a patient here." Then he considered what he'd just seen, what he'd seen at the pool earlier.

"Father Gabraulti was quite clear about it," she said.

Brad recognized an expectation more than an invitation. Gabraulti was no fool; he had been with Brad when he'd had his *episode* by the pool. Just a moment before Brad had questioned his own sanity. He had to accept that there was something wrong. He asked himself, was it more likely that he was being haunted by some other-worldly Leviathan bent on his torment, or that the stress of his traumatic accident and the unknown whereabouts of his family was causing him some sort of mental or emotional breakdown? He felt a little foolish that the answer to that question was so clear.

Sister Monica did not wait for him to respond. "Please follow me," was all she said.

The Sister rotated in place then began to glide out into the hall. Brad followed several feet behind. He marveled again at the strange smoothness of her motion. Watching the shiny floor in her wake he hoped to see some reflection beneath the hem of her black dress, some clue to this mundane mystery, but her tunic left no gap of light between it and the floor.

They passed the open door of the lounge and turned a corner in the corridor. Immediately, Brad could hear a voice speaking. It was a single boisterous voice he heard. He recognized it as Ray's, the snake-handling priest who'd murdered his flock. Brad felt his muscles tense after his earlier encounter with the big man. Then he saw light from a doorway down the hall and recognized it as the source of the voice and their destination.

Before reaching it, he noticed a much more prominent set of double doors at the end of the corridor. They were large, oak doors, reinforced with big iron rivets and hinges. They were doors that looked misplaced and mismatched to all the others he'd seen here.

Sister Monica stopped and turned to face Brad. Her wordless instruction confirmed their destination.

"What's with the big doors?" he asked, gesturing further down the hallway.

Only her eyes moved to address him. "That's the West Wing," she said. "It's of no concern this evening. Please step inside, Mr. Turner. Everyone is waiting."

He took another look at the doors. Antony had mentioned the West Wing as home to the most extreme residents of St. Lucius. The doors' sturdy appearance reinforced an impression that they locked something away.

Monster

Sister Monica cleared her throat. Brad nodded to her and did as he was asked.

He stood in the threshold for a moment and surveyed the new room. It was half the size of the lounge and had a ring of folding chairs in the center. There was a scarred wooden table against the far wall with a coffee maker, cups, and the usual trappings. There was no accompanying aroma, and the coffee maker did not appear to be plugged into an outlet. The walls were adorned only with broken plaster and exposed lath. Above, a single long florescent lighting fixture lit the room. It made the circle of chairs seem spotlighted and the periphery dark. The same shiny green marbled floor reflected the muted images of everything above. To Brad the room conjured the image of a stage set in an empty theater.

Brad recognized most everyone in the room from earlier in the day. He'd given them names in his head. There was the Witness, the Succubus, the Child Killer, and the Mass Murdering Priest. But there was another face that was not familiar. Here was a young man, a teenager, perhaps younger than that. He was thin, with sharp features, dark hair and eyes. Wearing jeans, a black hooded sweatshirt and high-top tennis shoes, he made no eye contact with anyone, just stared at the shiny floor. He seemed out of place among the group, but Brad guessed it was unlikely that they had a separate children's program here. Regardless of the addition, this was by far the strangest company he had ever kept. Maybe it was a mistake to come here, he thought.

Mr. Ray was lording over the group with his loud voice. Others stared into space or sat with eyes closed. Antony yawned. Ray went silent when he saw Brad. He locked eyes on him. Then just as suddenly he averted his gaze to the floor as Sister Monica stepped fully into the room. Brad could see Ray still staring at him through his reflection in the floor.

"Please have a seat, Mr. Turner," Sister Monica instructed.

There were a few empty seats in the circle. Antony looked up at him with a welcoming smile. He patted the empty chair beside him. Brad scanned the circle, then sat beside Antony. Antony nodded and smiled but remained silent. He appeared to be keeping his mouth shut. He looked excited as if waiting for his turn to speak.

Sister Monica glided over and pulled a chair out so that she sat just outside of the circle. She adjusted her tunic then folded her long boney hands in her lap. Even while seated, there was no sign of feet beneath her clothing. She silently skimmed the group with her eyes. "Who would like to begin?" she asked.

"You know he's going to ruin everything. He's got to choose a side. He's not even a believer," Ray said turning his face up to address Sister Monica. He sounded calm and respectful in her presence, but there was something underlying that seethed through his teeth. He was obviously talking about Brad.

"That's not a fair thing to say," Antony spoke up in defense of his new-found friend.

"Shut the fuck up, rat man." Ray raised his head and leaned forward when he addressed Antony. "Have you seen your boy today? Huh? Have you?"

Antony lowered his head and softened his tone. "That's not fair either."

Sister Monica looked at Ray. "Mr. Turner will only be with us a short time. You needn't worry about him. I think it would be more beneficial if you continued to explore your own issues. The key to modifying behavior is to identify its origins. The last time we talked, you seemed to have discovered some new insights. Why don't you share them with us?"

"But it's all related," he began. "And he's part of it too. Damned blasphemer. He'll be the ruin of us all."

"Raymond," she said sharply.

He lowered his head again. "Alright, alright, I know what you want me to say. I knew it was wrong. That's what you want to hear, right? I knew it from the start. But I had to listen... I'd have to do it again too. I didn't have a choice."

"Listen to who?" the Sister asked.

"You know exactly who!"

"These sessions are meant to help all of us, Raymond. Please, tell us what you mean."

"It was Him... you know who I mean. You don't have to pretend. That's why I did what I did."

As he spoke, he looked up and raised his shoulders up near his ears as if the ceiling might at any moment come down upon him. "At first, I didn't want to listen. You know that. They were my people. I was responsible for them. But He said I had to let them go, that I needed to set them free. I struggled. It didn't make sense. But how could I argue? It's not like I could disobey!"

"And how does it make you feel?" Monica asked. "That you listened to this message... or was it a command?"

"What do you think? Do you think I had a choice? I loved those people." His eyes began watering, and his nose began to run. "They were my friends and family, my parishioners. They believed as much as I did, with all their hearts. But He chose me, didn't He? I did what He asked. And now I'm waiting, stuck in this place. Waiting for *my* reward."

Ray looked up at Brad sitting across the circle from him. He nearly growled. "But now *he's* here. I was told about him - told he was coming. I don't know what He wants with him, but he's going to ruin everything. Now I'll never be free, never!"

Brad listened as Ray spoke. But his mind wandered. He imagined another place and time, clear as the room around them. Yet it was somehow more than imagined, Brad felt literally in another place. He saw Ray, thinner than he was now, dressed in his priests' outfit, black with white collar. He was standing behind an alter in a church. It was beautiful. The ornately carved wood of the alter matched the pews, the lectern, the candle strewn tabernacle. Thick wooden beams curved up around him like the inverted ribs of a sailing ship; they supported the high arched ceiling above. Behind him a collection of vibrant stained glass. In Ray's outstretched hands he cupped a chalice now empty.

Then Brad saw what was before him. On the floor, laid about the communion rail, were stacks of bodies. Men and boys in suits and ties, women with their daughters in their Sunday best. They lay intertwined, heaped upon each other. Each stained in a frothy foam vomited from their once living mouths. Many seemed to have embraced each other in their last moments of pain and torment. Brad could smell the acrid bile and deadly toxin that poisoned them. And Brad saw the look on Ray's face. It was not what he described to the group - it was a look of pure elation.

The image vanished as Ray spat out his last words. Brad barely heard what he was saying. He looked over at Sister Monica with raised brows as he snapped out of his vision.

Monica's voice retained its same emotionless quality. "Mr. Turner has his own burdens," she said to Ray. "You may be assured that they have no connection to you." She turned to Brad. "Mr. Turner, would you please enlighten the group. Tell us what brings you here. It may help to dispel this anxiety that Raymond is feeling. It's important that we converse in the spirit of openness. Would you please set everyone's mind at ease?"

Brad looked around the circle. All their eyes were upon him, except for the strange boy. Brad sensed a bizarre range of emotions - boredom from the Watcher, excitement from Antony, lust from the Succubus, anger from Ray. He also understood quite clearly that Sister Monica would not let him escape this circle without participating.

"Well," he began awkwardly. "There was an accident, I guess you'd call it that. I was driving with my wife, Sarah, and our son, Jason. There was a storm; it came up out of nowhere. I'd never seen anything like it. It rained so hard that I had to pull the car over. The next thing we knew, water started to rise. It must have been a flash flood or something. I hadn't realized it, of course it was dark, but we must have been in a depression, some kind of low spot along the road, a ravine, a natural drainage. I don't know. The water came up so fast that we couldn't pull out. The engine died. We were stuck."

Brad's chest squeezed with pressure again. His anxiety built as he re-lived the experience. Like his vision of Ray presiding over his congregation of poisoned corpses, he could see himself struggling to deal with the terror of the rising waters. It was like he was watching it all unfold again, floating above it, but not being able to intervene. And the screaming, he could hear Jason screaming. It cut him like razor claws digging into his brain.

"We tried to get out of the car. I climbed out first so that I could take the baby. But it was too late. The water rose so fast. And everything was gone. It was the strangest thing. It was like I was all alone in the world. There was nothing. I can't explain it!"

"Is that when you saw It?" Ray accused more than asked.

Brad stopped suddenly. He knew exactly what Ray was talking about. But that was impossible. Brad wasn't sure he'd seen anything at all. It was all part of his imagination. That feeling of presence. That raw power that he imagined he felt was just a mental trick, the personification of his own weakness and helplessness. The Leviathan was just something his mind had made up to help him deal with his loss and guilt. It wasn't real. Brad tried his best to ignore the comment.

"The next thing I knew, I was here," he said. "It all must have happened near here, the storm, the flood, the accident. It's all blank. But my family, Oh God. I don't know. They're out there, somewhere. I have to hope that they're alive. That someone found them and maybe they're looking for me. Or maybe they're in a different place, another hospital nearby. They wouldn't have been brought here. That's why this place... I mean, I'm grateful, but I need to get out of here. I need to look for them, even if they're..." He couldn't bring himself to finish the sentence.

"And you will be on your way soon enough," Sister Monica said to him. She shifted her attention back to Ray. "You see Raymond, Mr. Turner being here has nothing to do with you. He is simply a guest by chance. Like us all, he must deal with his own suffering. As children of the Almighty it is our duty to ease that suffering, not to cause further distress. We must all do what is asked of us if we seek final redemption. Isn't that right Mr. Turner?"

She did not turn when she addressed him.

Brad was caught off guard. This religious talk made him a little more uncomfortable than he already felt. He chided himself for being surprised. Of course, he knew that Saint Lucius Sanitarium had a religious affiliation. Christ, it was staffed by nuns and a priest. He'd be stupid not to know that. The truth was, he didn't know much about religion. No more than he'd learned from a lifetime of T.V. and movies and from living with Sarah.

Brad was not brought up with religion. It wasn't until he got to middle school that he started to realize that other kids went to church and believed in a god. He remembered how the idea intrigued him then. It was cooler than Santa Claus. But like believing in the jolly old elf, Brad grew out of it. Having never experienced the indoctrination of religion, the concept faded from his mind without struggle or thought. Like believing that kissing girls gave you "cooties", maturity replaced the thought with reality, and he was never tempted to re-examine the belief.

That is not to say that he didn't know *anything* about religion. He was aware that Christianity had many branches, he knew who Jesus was and that he was a Jew. He understood that Islam was another offshoot of the same general idea of God, that its historical roots sprang from the same ground, but that it had its own independent claims of magic and miracles. Brad didn't quite understand what all the fuss was about. In his mind, they all believed in the same God, they just disagreed about the details.

Then there were other religions. He thought the Buddhists were pretty cool, and the Hindu reincarnation thing too. Coming back as an animal sounded great if you could pick one yourself. He thought he'd like to be an eagle, or maybe a bear, like a grizzly bear or a polar bear. Only with his luck, he'd wind up a slug.

Then there was the classical stuff, like the Greek gods and the Norse gods. Those were the most fun. He knew them mostly from comic books and action movies.

But in the end, Brad respected that everyone had their own thing, and so long as they didn't force it on him, he didn't care what people did with their own time. The Bible had no more impact on his life than *The Odyssey* or *The Iliad*.

Sister Monica was facing him now, waiting for a response.

"I'm sorry," Brad said. "What was that?"

"We are all looking to be saved," she paraphrased herself. "Isn't that right?"

Put that way, Brad was in full agreement. "Yeah, I suppose that's true."

"Ha," someone said.

Brad saw that it was Edith, the woman he'd come to think of as the Witness. This was the first sign she had shown that she was even aware of what was going on around her.

"Edith?" Sister Monica began. "Do you have something to add?"

"Not everyone gets saved," she said. "You know that as well as I. I've seen what happens, I know better."

"Yes, Edith, you're right," said Monica. "There is only one road that leads to salvation. We must surrender ourselves to the Almighty. Only by giving up everything do we gain eternal life. It's a choice only the faithful can make, but it must be from the heart. We reap only what we sow."

Brad didn't like the implication there. He started to squirm a little. It was one thing to go along with the crowd, but he could read between the lines. Either get with the program or miss out on the prize. Except that missing out on the prize sounded like it was pretty bad. She was talking about Hell. He understood what Hell was supposed to be like, fire and brimstone, endless torment, and torture. Even in the best case, if it was not a physical place, it was a mental state of endless suffering, one that his experiences of the last few days had become easier to imagine. For the first time in his life, he understood in a real sense, that people had actual fear of damnation, and he pitied them that belief.

"This is all a bunch of crap."

Brad heard the Succubus speak up. A tinge of guilt accompanied the term. Perhaps it was his own self-defense mechanism. Up to this point he had intentionally tried not to look at her, but now he was forced to admit that she was very attractive. Hearing that she was a sex addict, imagining the acts described by Antony, he could feel something within him. He could see himself engaged with her in lewd acts of depravity. He couldn't help himself. She was the kind of woman that had been mostly out of his reach. And he knew from his own experience that her type was trouble. Even so, she inspired thoughts that he hadn't had for Sarah in a long time. Again, he was reminded of damnation.

Everyone was looking at Mary. As attractive as she was, right now her defiant attitude animated her face.

"I mean for Christ's sake, that's all we ever talk about," she said. "As if any of us have a chance of salvation. You're all a bunch of freakin' psychos. You think that just because you say you're sorry, all will be forgiven. That's not the world I've been living in. And anyway, how does that even make sense. Like Ray's going to get into Heaven after what he's done, just because he feels bad. Boo fuckin' Hoo."

Ray shifted in his seat.

"How is that even fair to people that don't do fucked up shit?" She pointed at Brad now. "Look at new guy over there. He's just looking for his family, thinking something terrible happened to them. That ain't fair. What'd he do to deserve that? Now look at him, stuck in here with the rest of us."

She focused completely on Brad. "You need to get the fuck out of this place, and you can take me with you. I never hurt anybody. Not like these psychos."

"Mary," Sister Monica addressed her with that strong, calm, and commanding tone of hers. "It's very kind of you to empathize with Mr. Turner, but you know better than to involve others in your own issues. After all, wasn't it your questionable interactions with others that brought you here to begin with?"

Mary looked at Sister Monica. She curled up her face and clamped her mouth.

Brad leaned slowly back in his seat trying to be invisible. His face felt warm, and his heart beat rapid. He was too close to the epicenter of tension in the room.

Next, the boy stood up from his chair. He looked at Brad but remained silent. He was younger than Brad had first guessed. Maybe he was twelve years old, maybe ten. Brad didn't know. He couldn't imagine the boy getting much therapeutic benefit from the group, not as he had just watched it evolve. The boy's face was downturned, his shoulders slumped, his movement looked painful. He slowly shuffled across the circle and found an opening between vacant chairs. Brad turned his head following him as he walked through the door and out into the hallway.

"You saw that didn't you?" Antony said to Brad.

"Excuse me," Brad answered.

"The boy, he just walked across the room and out the door! You saw him, didn't you?" Antony was overly excited.

"Yeah?" Brad answered. "I was wondering who he was. I didn't see him earlier in the lounge."

Antony leaped manic from his chair. He pointed around at the group. "See, I told you! Nobody believed me, but I told you!"

"What? What are you talking about?"

Sister Monica stood up. "I think we've had enough for tonight," she said. "You are all excused to your rooms."

The rest of the group stood up and started toward the door. Ray was grumbling and giving Brad a sideways glance. Brad remained seated so that the room could clear.

"Wait! Where are you going? Come on, this is important." Antony addressed them. "He saw him, he said he saw him."

"Mr. Sharpe!" Monica commanded.

Antony went silent as a beaten dog. He looked at Brad, his eyes silently begging him to reaffirm his experience. Then he stomped defeated from the room in a quiet tantrum.

Finally, Brad stood up beside Sister Monica. "What was that about? What's got him so excited?"

"Mr. Sharpe suffers from recurring hallucinations," she said. "It's an issue he's been working through in therapy. I'm sure you meant well, but I'd admonish you not to play into his fantasies."

"Wait a minute, I still don't get it. What are you talking about?"

"Mr. Sharpe believes that his murdered son is still with him. He claims to see him wandering the facility. It's not unusual given the trauma of his loss, but it's also not healthy for him to hold on to the past. He needs to move on. I should have warned you beforehand about some of our patients' histories so that you would not inadvertently disturb anyone. It's my fault. Perhaps tomorrow we can sit down and have a little talk about the residents."

Brad stood dumbfounded. He had started to suspect that there was something wrong with him. He too had seen things, things that couldn't be real. But how could it be possible that he was sharing in the hallucinations of others. That was crazy. But he had seen the boy, even if he hadn't understood who he was. Antony had seen him too. But what of everyone else? That boy was real. That was the truth of it. Maybe everybody was in on some appalling secret. Maybe Mal was right, maybe no one here could be trusted.

Brad followed the logic. If Antony's dead son were here, alive and taunting his accused father, then maybe there was something more to Brad's arrival here. And maybe someone knew more about his own family than they were saying. Brad kept these thoughts to himself. He tried to disguise his growing mistrust. Was someone trying to make him feel like he was losing it? Had he been drugged? Why would they do that? He smiled at Sister Monica.

"I think I'll head back to my room," he said. "It's been a long day and I'd like to get some sleep. Good night Sister."

"Good night Mr. Turner," she answered. "Perhaps it would be best if you remained in your room for the night. We don't want any mishaps."

"No, of course not," he responded. "Good night."

Chapter Five

Jason was born in April. It snowed that day. Sarah's parents had come to town a few days before to await their grandson's arrival and were with them at the hospital for the happy event. Brad was a wreck. He never felt so alone and useless. He knew that her parents did not approve of him. He was under-employed with few prospects. He didn't attend church. He had even failed to marry their daughter and make her a so-called "honest woman". He couldn't explain to them the circumstances behind that decision; he thought that was Sarah's place. What she told her parents was her business.

Start to finish, labor lasted over twelve hours. He was told he should be grateful that it went so fast. To him those hours stretched into an eternity. As he watched Sarah go through the pain, he marveled at how anyone could survive such torment. Why would anyone choose to go through it? Especially women who had more than one child. The first time you could convince yourself that it wouldn't be as bad as it looked, but once you'd experienced that sensation, the cramping pain of contractions, the ripping and tearing of the body, the final surge of something erupting from the body far larger than the ill-designed orifice made to release it - it was insanity. After watching this with his own eyes he did not feel the joy of fatherhood. He was nauseous and repulsed.

Laying there afterwards, Sarah held her newborn son, naked against her breast. Brad saw the absolute manifestation of love and joy that was motherhood, but he felt only numbness and loss. He saw a future now determined and an infinite hallway of doors being shut forever. He accepted his new path. He would do what was expected of him. He would not complain. But the realization of the moment flooded his mind. He did not know the same elation that he saw on Sarah's face, even though he had expected it, hoped for it. He stood quiet, his head hung low, and wondered how these feelings could have evaded him. Because of this, he smiled and said nothing, and the crushing weight of guilt sat heavy upon his chest. Gently smoothing the sweaty hair from Sarah's brow, he leaned over and kissed her forehead, then stepped out of the way for her parents.

Now, a year later, Brad lay on his back staring at the ceiling. He couldn't sleep; his mind was racing too fast. The worst thing that could ever happen had already come true. He'd lost his family. He cursed himself for failing to protect them and for letting things get so out of control. If only he had reacted faster, made different choices. Maybe if he had gone a little further down the road before pulling off. What if he had sent Sarah out of the car first and then handed Jason to her. He would gladly have sacrificed himself if it meant saving them. The second guessing was driving him mad.

And that madness was in his thoughts too. He wondered if he was losing his mind.

First, there was the missing time. How had he gotten from the roof of his car, spinning helplessly on the flood waters, to appearing at this archaic home for the forgotten stepchildren of a Christian god? And what was this horrible creature, this Leviathan, whose speechless, heartless presence weighed on his subconscious and waking mind like impending doom? Brad was no psychiatrist, but he understood that the mind had self-defense mechanisms. Sometimes it built walls for protection, or it created stories to justify the most horrific events or behaviors. That much made sense to him. He decided that this creature was the symbol of events for which he had no control, events that left him powerless, helpless, and afraid.

But there were other things. The strange creatures he saw in the garden, his memory of them seemed more vivid than his actual experience. He could almost hear the creaking of their long appendages encased in hard plated exoskeletons. He could imagine the gooey green slime that flowed through those large soulless bodies. But they too seemed born from his memories. They were reflections of inhuman crawly things that lived in the dark reaches of the world he knew. What they might symbolize or why his mind might conjure them, he did not know. Still, he was sure that they held some meaning, however disturbing they might be. An itchy, crawling sensation creeped up his spine at the mere thought of them.

The more he tried to justify these things, the more convenient seemed the explanations. The puzzle pieces fit too easily. With his armchair psychology, he could place his simple layman's labels where they belonged. Still, there was an otherworldly atmosphere that encompassed everything he was experiencing, this place, the people, his visions. It was more like a dream state, or nightmare more likely.

Maybe this was all a dream. He'd seen that deus ex machina trope used in countless movies. The hero runs a gambit of horrible adventures only to discover at the end that it was all a dream. He decided to test this hypothesis. Lying in bed he slapped himself across the face as hard as he could. The strike was jarring and the sting of flesh upon flesh intense. However, he did not wake from any subliminal reality. He lay there with only a fresh red handprint on his cheek and the acceptance that his nightmare seemed real enough.

He began to wonder if his most recent surprise might be the key he was searching for. The boy he'd seen at the group session was no ethereal monster swimming through a dark and haunted void, nor was he some bizarre insect fingering up his spinal column. He was something real, something that could exist in the real world. Brad did not believe in ghosts, and shared hallucinations were beyond what he accepted as possible. If his belief in the boys' reality were true, then the boy must be here in the building. He could be found. If he could be found, then Brad could uncover some truth about what was happening. He might discover why someone would torture poor Antony by making him believe that he'd murdered his son. And if someone went through the trouble to deceive Antony, then what other lies might Brad uncover? Maybe they were lying to him about how he'd gotten there, or even about what had happened to his family. If Antony's son were here, then maybe, just maybe, he might hope that his family were here too, alive somewhere in this dilapidated hulk of a building. These were answers he had to have.

Brad couldn't get the image of Antony's son out of his mind. Although he was certain that he had never seen him before, it was uncanny how familiar he seemed. He reminded Brad of a kid he had known when he was in Middle School. What was that boy's name? Tommy - Tommy Perkins. That's right. Tommy lived two blocks over from Brad in the same neighborhood. Tommy was his first best friend, maybe the only real friend that Brad had ever had. How could he have forgotten? Maybe because of what happened to Tommy. Their friendship was short-lived.

Brad reached back to the day the two of them met. It was near the end of summer vacation, a blistering hot summer. On the corner of Overcrest Road and Stevenson Lane there was a huge boxwood bush; it provided perfect cover from the house whose property it sat on. Brad remembered sitting on that curb on those hot lonely days. The late summer sun would bake the black asphalt on the road's edge, and right along the curb the hot tar gave rise to tiny black rubbery bubbles. Each day they would rise anew in the wavering heat. Brad liked to sit and pop them with his fingers. The good ones filled with hot water and if he popped them just right, he could shoot tiny streams of scalding liquid out toward the road and watch them evaporate on the hot surface. If he were unlucky, the water would shoot backward or to the side and burn his hands. It was a game of chicken he played with himself, testing his courage. At eleven years old it seemed like a brave and adventurous game to play.

It was on one of these days that Tommy appeared. He'd come walking around the big boxwood and stopped short, wide-eyed and mouth agape. Brad remembered thinking how funny that expression was as he looked up at him from the curb. Tommy was a skinny kid, tall for his age. He wore a red shirt and Bermuda shorts. Brad thought he saw Tommy's knees shake. Of course, Brad had his own spike of adrenaline rushing through his limbs, startled in the moment. There was only one thing he could think to say.

"Wanna pop some bubbles?"

They spent the rest of that summer hanging out together. They both rode Schwinn bicycles with banana seats and roamed endlessly around the neighborhood. They impressed each other by pulling wheelies and riding with no hands. Sometimes they ventured to the small plot of woods that bordered the furniture assembly plant where Brad's father worked. They would explore the tiny stream there looking for small snakes and tiny frogs. These became fewer and fewer as they approached the boy-sized drainage tunnel emerging from a slope among the trees.

The stacked- stone entrance was covered with an ancient cast iron gate. Neither of them had the nerve to squeeze between the bars and wander inside, instead they shouted into its dark throat, listening to the echoes of their voices. And when they were silent, they could hear the echo of cave crickets living deep in its damp hollow passage.

On the hottest days they would hang out at Brad's house. Brad remembered how happy his mother had been to see that Brad had a friend. It was a strange kind of happiness, one mixed with a breed of sadness that he'd only seen in grown-ups.

He and Tommy played video games and watched horror movies from Brad's collection. Sometimes they even broke out Brad's G.I. Joe action figures and made up their own adventures. This was all new to Tommy. He wasn't allowed to play video games. He wasn't allowed to watch television unless he was supervised by his mom. Tommy's parents were strict about that kind of thing.

They didn't play at Tommy's house much that summer. Tommy's house had a strange vibe. The thing Brad remembered most about Tommy's house were the crosses and portraits hanging on their walls. The pictures were all the same, a guy with long hair and a beard - it was Jesus. Brad guessed that he probably knew that at the time. Some were just of his face, looking all peaceful and stuff, others showed him being killed. Someone had actually taken this guy and nailed his hands and feet to a big piece of wood. It was gross. It was also really weird that someone would hang that image in their home, especially with kids around. The pictures made Tommy's house feel dark, and like they were always being watched. Brad remembered looking over his shoulder, thinking he might catch the painted eyes moving. Tommy's house always felt like the principal's office.

Tommy told him the story about Jesus, how he had brought guys back from the dead, and how the Jews had killed him for it. And then how he himself had also come back from the dead. It didn't seem so far out to Brad. He had horror movies in his collection that were kind of like that. The difference was that Tommy and his folks believed that it was all true. Tommy even had an uncle who worked as a priest at the church they belonged too. His name was Uncle Mike. Brad had only seen him a couple of times. Tommy didn't talk about Uncle Mike. Brad couldn't blame him for that. It seemed weird that a grown-up would focus their whole life on some super-old dead guy, especially one who could do magic stuff like in the movies.

Monster

As different as that all seemed, none of it bothered Brad. Even at eleven years old he realized that people believed all sorts of things. There were people on T.V. that believed in Bigfoot and the Loch Ness Monster and space aliens. So, believing in Jesus seemed kind of tame to him. Besides, Tommy and his family were nice enough people, and Tommy was his best friend.

It was odd that he would be thinking of Tommy right now. So many years had passed. Tommy looked nothing like the boy he was looking for. But perhaps it was the look he saw on the face of Antony's son, that lone emptiness. He'd seen that look on Tommy's face too. He'd never realized how deeply that look had affected him, even after so much time. If he could find Antony's son, if he could help him, then maybe in some karmic sense, he would be helping Tommy too.

In the present moment, Brad sat up in bed and looked around his dark room. He wondered what time it was. How long he had lay there thinking? He guessed it was late in the middle of the long night. Slipping into his pants and shoes, he crept to the door and slowly cracked it open. The hallway was lit, but not bright. Only a third of the light banks along the ceiling were turned on and as before, some of their florescent tubes buzzed and flickered. No one was about. Brad decided that everyone must be fast asleep, but stealth was important if he wanted to explore the building in search of Antony's son.

Once in the hallway he decided that the lower level was where he should begin his search. It was further away from the rooms occupied by his strange housemates. If someone were hiding, or being hidden, they were likely buried far and deep from the others. If the lower level proved to be vacant, then he would have to turn to the heavy wooden doors that led to the

West Wing. Brad hoped he wouldn't have to find a way through them. There was something about that passage that twisted his gut. Maybe it was Antony's caution that the West Wing was home to St. Lucius' most dangerous residents. That they might be more dangerous than the residents he'd already met was disturbing enough, but there was something else, something less discernable that radiated with warning. There was something beyond those doors that he did not want to see.

Brad made his way to the stairwell leading down. He came out into the lobby where he was initially concealed by the large square columns. Using them as cover he quietly surveyed the open room. He could see the desk where Sister Kayla sat as gatekeeper earlier in the day. A small desk lamp with a green glass shade was the only source of light for the large room. The desk was unoccupied now. There was no one in sight. Brad moved into the open and could see the doors that led to the outside world. The glass was dark.

He walked over and stood beside the desk. It was pristine; the sign-in book sat open revealing only blank pages. Brad spotted the rotary phone sitting there and couldn't help himself. He picked up the receiver and held it to his ear. At first there was only silence, no dial tone at all. But then he began to hear a faint soft reverberation. It was like a light breeze or a distant whimper. Then it became a chorus of whispers. He couldn't make them out, as faint as they were, not even the strange language that he thought he heard. But there was something about the sound, like a dirge so profound that it touched him in a moment of utter despair. He hung up the receiver harder than he intended.

He stepped around the desk and opened the single drawer. Inside was a stack of stationary, a few spare pencils and pens, paperclips, a stapler, a set of keys. A small flashlight rolled with the movement of the drawer. Brad picked it up, twisted the lens-cap and it came on. He scanned the lobby with it, then turned it off and slipped it into his pocket.

Opposite the front doors and foyer was the hall which he had toured with Father Gabraulti. It yawned before him like a long dark tunnel bored into the body of the facility. Brad walked slowly toward it and stopped. He took a moment to let his eyes adjust. A few doors along its length stood ajar. They let in enough light from unseen windows to illuminate the corridor a fraction above complete black. He steadied his nerves and delved into the dark passage.

Even in the near pitch he was aware of his shadowy reflection following him in the floor. It tweaked his anxiety in a way that made it seem as if it were not his own. He tried to ignore the impression. The rubber soles of his shoes made soft padding sounds in the silence. In other circumstances his footfalls would have been unremarkable, but here they betrayed his every step. Some doors facing the interior side of the building stood open. Their darkness so deep that nothing penetrated their portals. His neck and shoulders tightened painfully in response. Each one Brad passed filled his imagination, that something waited just within, ready at any moment to reach out and touch him. He held the flashlight fumbling in his pocket, fighting the desire to illuminate his path, but he didn't want to give himself away or whitewash his night vision. He gritted his teeth and clenched his jaw.

Soon he came to the alcove where the steel doors barred the way into the basement level. Like the wooden doors to the West Wing above him, this was a landmark that held a similar revulsion. These doors held something in rather than kept him out. He stepped close and pressed his palm against the metal. Instead of the cold that he expected, he felt warmth. It thawed the blood flowing through his capillaries and made him shiver. He imagined for a moment that Mal Livengood was somewhere below, stoking the flaming furnace, standing silhouetted in the light of heat and fire. Brad took hold of the warm door handle and tugged. The doors resisted. They were locked.

As Brad took a step backward, he heard a noise rise from the low dark corner of the alcove. He froze in place. He recognized the sound at once but dared not move for fear of stepping on its source. So out of place, he thought that he must have been mistaken. He fumbled for the flashlight in his pocket and twisted it to life. Shining the beam at the floor beside him confirmed his suspicion. Sitting on the polished floor right in front of him, no bigger than his own fist, was a frog. Its large bulbous eyes stared up at him unaffected by the light. It let out another long-extended croak.

Brad took a slow step backward, but his foot bumped into something. The flashlight beam followed his eyes to the tiny obstruction. It was another frog. A croak came from further to his right. Then the sensation of movement all around set his mind spinning. His ears filled with the sound of croaking frogs. He scanned the floor and saw dozens and dozens of them surrounding him. They seemed to have manifested from out of the darkness itself. He held back a moan standing in their midst. Their bodies appeared slimy and covered in infected growths. Some of them were split open and oozing. They leaped about and squirmed and crawled over each other in a congealing mass.

Repulsed and nauseous, his eyes wide and darting, Brad moved backward again. This time he slid his feet over the crowded floor to push himself away rather than risk stepping on and crushing their fragile bloated bodies. They bounced against his legs as they threw themselves directionless in the air. He backed away watching them in the narrow field of his light. There were hundreds now. In their center they were piled two feet thick in a growing, churning amphibian orgy. Their raucous croaks and screams attacked his ears.

Now in the clear, he turned and rushed away down the short corridor. He imagined them growing in an enormous wave, rising behind him, ready to overwhelm and cover him drowning below.

He saw the opaque glass doors of the pool room in front of him now. They glowed dim in the surrounding darkness. Brad rushed through and closed them behind him. He stopped with his back bracing them closed, gasping in quick breaths.

The loud cacophony of croaking frogs had suddenly ceased, and he was in silence now. The glass ceiling above the pool let in angles of moonlight which lit much of the large room. Brad turned off his flashlight and slipped it back into his pocket. Like the lobby area, the pool room had large square columns holding up the roof. There were wide rectangular walkways raised on the outside perimeter of the room. These areas were in shadow, but Brad could see openings in the walls that must have led to changing rooms and showers. The smell of chlorine was strong. He closed his eyes to let them readjust to the darkness again.

When he opened them, he stepped away from the doors and toward the pool. He avoided looking in its dark waters; he remembered too well his vision of the flood and the return of the Leviathan. But he tried to resurrect some form of rational thought. He tried to remember his self-counseling belief that his mind was full of self-delusion and that discovering the truth was the only way to confront whatever was happening in his head.

It may have been his eyes adjusting to the dark. Maybe the moon was breaking free of cloud cover somewhere high above the glass ceiling. But the waters of the pool began to brighten. He could see the lines painted at the bottom shimmering below. He began to see the blue of the water and the rippling effect of light dancing on the walls and columns around him. The vision mesmerized and frightened in equal parts.

Brad raised his eyes to the far side of the room. Across the long stretch of the pool, he saw the distant wall of glass panels. They were black with only hints of the garden beyond, but they reflected the pool room back at him. The waters glowed blue as if the sub-surface lights were turned on. He could see the tiled columns marching away in reflected perspective. At the far edge of his sight, he could see the opaque doors he had just come through. It was then that he noticed the omission. His own reflection was missing from the scene.

He looked down at himself, touched his chest to confirm his existence. His eyes darted back to the far reflection. He was immediately relieved to see the human figure now mirrored there. But with further scrutiny he saw that the figure was standing back just inside of the entrance doors. Brad squinted, trying to force his eyes to focus on the dark figure. Then he saw it step forward and confirmed this was not his own reflection. Brad's heart pounded in his chest. His limbs froze like stone. They refused to turn and face whatever approached him. He forced his will to respond. Moving his body was like rolling a heavy boulder, but he managed to twist around and plant his feet.

The figure slowly moving toward him was big and broad. It slipped from the deep shadow and into the faint light of the pool waters. It was Raymond. Even from ten paces away Brad was dwarfed by his size. All Brad could make out clearly was his face. Raymond's chin was down, and he wore a horrible scowl. His unblinking eyes stared at Brad with distain. The rest of his body was cloaked in shadow, but there was movement there that made him seem as if he lacked solidity. He seemed to pulse and squirm.

"What do you want?" Brad's voice came out shakier than he'd hoped.

"I'm here for you," Raymond growled. "I've waited too long and I'm not going to let you fuck things up."

"I don't know what you're talking about," Brad said. "I told you, I'm just here until I can get a ride, until I can find my family. I'm not messing with you. I don't want any trouble."

"You think it matters what you want," Raymond said. "*He* set all this in motion. *He* made me lead my people away. Do you think I wanted to do that? And what was my reward? I'm here, stuck here waiting, abandoned, forsaken. Now *He* brings *you* here? You don't worship *Him*, you don't believe. You've got to be kidding me, right? Is everything I've done for nothing? Well, I'll show *Him*. I'll make sure you don't have a choice!"

Ray took another step forward and Brad could see him now for what he was. His body squirmed in unnatural motion. His clothes were filled with snakes. Serpents tangled and writhed under his shirt, around his legs beneath his pants. Some slithered out from the collar around his neck then dove back under cover. Ray didn't seem to notice. It was like his body was made of snakes, a heaping pile of intertwined serpents squirming to hold his shape together and move according to his will. He stepped forward reaching for Brad. His fingers were individual snakes with tiny snapping jaws and spitting tongues.

Brad stumbled and caught his foot on the edge of the pool. He fell backward in a bizarre moment of slow motion. There was a loud whooshing sound. He expected to hit the cold water, but instead he continued to fall. He hit hard on the dry concrete of the pool bottom.

He lay there a moment on his back, then lifted on his elbows. He looked around in disbelief of his own eyes. The pool waters had parted. He lay in a narrow channel that ran down the lengthwise center of the pool. On either side of him, just beyond his reach, the water had lifted to form walls taller than the surrounding pools' perimeter edge. The walls swayed and rippled with surface tension but held in place by some invisible force that went beyond explanation. The waters retained their unnatural glow and Brad could see through to the sides of the pool and the columns that surrounded it. Then he saw Ray, his writhing form at the pool edge, beginning to descend the steps between the partitioned waters.

Brad crawled backward on his elbows, scraping them against the concrete. He flipped over and rushed down slope toward the deep end. Ray was moving slowly and methodically, but he was close behind. Brad could hear the slithering and hissing of the approaching reptilian mass. The pool bottom was just ahead of him, a dead end. But it was sloped steeply back up to the high edge. Brad did not slow. He ran up the wall as far as he could and jumped. He caught the bull-nosed concrete lip of the pool and scrambled with his feet to pull himself up. At the last moment before being clutched by Rays' constricting grasp, Brad pulled his feet over the edge and rolled away.

"You won't get away that easy!" Ray shouted up at him. "You won't escape this place!"

Brad sprang to his feet. His body pumping a blast of adrenaline. Not for a moment did he believe that the threat was over. He looked down into the dry channel below him, breathing hard.

"You won't escape!" Ray repeated. "As God is my witness, there is no escape. Not for you, not for me, not for any of us! There is no choice but the one that's made for us!"

At that moment, whatever force that manipulated the water, released its power. Like a bursting dam the water walls collapsed. Tons of weight and pressure converged on Ray, slamming him from both sides. In the churning chaos he appeared to break apart into a thousand snakes, panicked and confused, wriggling in every direction. They vanished. Now Brad could see Ray beneath the water, even through the turbulence he could see that Ray once again had a human body with human limbs. He seemed disoriented - lost, he turned his face up and forced himself toward the surface. Just as he reached the top his face hit an invisible barrier. His nose bent sideways and erupted with blood. For just an instant, through the swirling red cloud, Brad thought he saw the face of Tommy's Uncle Mike.

Brad moved without thinking. He rushed forward and knelt at the water's edge. He leaned forward to reach under and grab his antagonist, but his hand met a solid surface. His fingertips screamed with pain from the collision, like he'd just slammed them into a solid wall. The pool water appeared as it should; it still waved back and forth from the calamity of its fallen walls. But something about its splashing surface created an impenetrable film, liquid flexibility with iron strength.

Ray was right below him. He banged on his side of the barrier, air bubbles rose from his mouth and nostrils with the muffled sounds of his cries for help. He began to claw his way backward toward the middle of the pool searching for some opening. Brad followed him. On hands and knees, Brad crawled out over the pool. If not for the wavering surface it would have been like crossing a clear sheet of ice on a frozen pond in rescue of a drowning skater, but as it was, it felt more like crawling across an enormous transparent bag of water. This reality where he did not sink was just as bizarre as Ray not being able to break its plain.

Brad cried out. "Help! Somebody help!"

He stood up on the water's surface and looked around. On the shadowy wall at the side of the room he spotted a pool cleaning net with its characteristic long pole. He rushed across the water onto the tiled floor, grabbed the net, and came back to the pool. Ray was right below him. He floated on his back barely below the water. He had stopped moving. No more bubbles of air rose from his water-logged lungs. His eyes were bulging; a shocked expression etched his face.

Brad stood looking down at him; he pumped with adrenaline. Standing on the edge, he held the net with the long pole pointing down. He stabbed and pounded at the surface just above Ray, but he could not pierce the barrier. He cried out again, stopped, frozen in the pose of a spear hunter about to skewer a fish from a lake.

Monster

The interior lights of the room suddenly snapped on. Brad winced from the brightness, momentarily blinded.

"What's going on in here?" came a familiar voice.

Brad turned his head squinting in the florescence. Just inside the room beside the bank of light switches was Mal Livengood. He was dressed in his green custodian's uniform. He casually walked from the doors to the side of the pool. He looked at the body now floating at the water's surface and then at Brad still frozen in his huntsman's stance.

"My goodness," Mal said. "Now that's a surprise." He reached out and wrapped his hand around the net pole. "Here, why don't you let me take that."

Brad released it. He stood like a mannequin, his mouth voiceless, stunned and suddenly aware of what this looked like. It must have appeared that he had killed Ray, attacked him with the pole, broken his nose with it, and somehow held him under with it until he drowned. Only Mal's arrival had kept him from a final jabbing blow. How could Mal see it any other way? And what could Brad say to deny it? No one would believe what had really happened. He didn't believe it himself.

Mal walked over to hang the net back in place. He whistled a faint tune as he replaced it on the wall.

Brad's mind was reeling once again. His neck muscles twitched, and his eyes blinked sporadic.

Mal came back and stood beside him.

"Why don't you head back up to your room," he suggested with a kind smile. "I'll take care of this." There was no judgment or blame in his voice, only what Brad took to be a calm concern. It was as if he'd volunteered to clean up the spilled drink of a drunken guest. "Get some rest. I'll see you in the morning." He continued to smile and patted Brads' back.

Christopher Cunningham

In a daze of exhaustion, stinging with adrenaline, on the verge of shock, Brad stumbled back from the edge of the pool and headed toward the doors.

Chapter Six

Brad passed through the doors of the pool room and out into the hallway. His mind was jumbled with images of what had just happened. He was going mad, he thought. No, he was already mad. What other explanation was there? On balance, he wished that the unbelievable things he'd seen *were* real. That a plague of frogs had issued-in the appearance of Ray, a maniac whose body was a living tangle of slithering snakes, and that the pool had parted like the Red Sea and engulfed and drowned his enemy. This horrific fantasy was more desirable than the alternative; that he had confronted his aggressor in the dark pool room and beaten him nearly to death with the pole of a pool net and left him to drown.

He couldn't explain why Mal had reacted the way he had. Maybe it was his way of diverting Brad's attention, of keeping him calm. If Mal were afraid that Brad might attack him as well, then maybe it was smart to act as if nothing were wrong. Perhaps Mal was now waiting in the pool room for Brad to get back to his room, so he could awaken the rest of the staff and make some plan to deal with Brad's homicidal impulse. That made sense to Brad's rational mind. But there was something about Mal that made Brad doubt the truth of his own justification. If Mal were acting or scheming, then he deserved an award for his performance.

Brad forced himself to assume the worst. He had just killed a man. His motive was self-defense. It must have been. Ray had been threatening him. There were witnesses to that. And Ray was a big guy, much larger and stronger than Brad. Anyone with eyes could see how mismatched a confrontation would be between the two of them. Plus, Ray was an admitted murderer. He had killed a church full of people. How he had wound up here and not in prison was a mystery, but irrelevant now. Who could blame Brad for protecting himself? It was insane - he was insane.

Even if the circumstances were different, Brad could claim insanity as a defense. After everything he'd been through, how could he not make that argument? Of course, he might end up permanently in a place like St. Lucius. Locked away in a mental ward for a crime committed in involuntary fantasy. His only hope to be released into the prison system to pay his dues to society. What had society ever done for him, he wondered?

But then a new dilemma. Whether he had committed this crime or not, it meant he would have to deal with the police, and lawyers, courts, hospitals, and prisons. It wasn't the first time he had thought about such things. But where did that leave his search for his family and the mystery of what had happened to them. Would he be blamed for that too? Would they assume that having killed Ray, that he had also killed his family?

Could they convict him of that without finding their bodies? For what else might he take the blame?

His panicked mind was taking him a step too far. His family wasn't dead. If he was wrong about that, then nothing else would matter. This line of thought brought his mind back into focus. He had started this night trying to find Antony's son, and in doing that, he hoped to find some clue about his family as well. Maybe it was a fool's errand, but he had time. There was no way to contact the police, at least not right away. Now their isolation would work in his favor. Maybe there was something else going on, something far more sinister than he could imagine. He needed to get back on track. He needed to find the boy.

His eyes now fully adjusted to the dark, he began back down the hall. He was familiar with this part of the facility. This short corridor led to an intersection. Straight ahead he'd find the alcove to Mal's basement hideaway, a left turn led back to the lobby, and the right turn remained unexplored. As he approached, he listened anxiously for the sound of croaking frogs, but he heard only silence interrupted by his own soft padding footsteps.

After a few moments he realized that something was wrong. He did not come to the intersection he expected. Instead, the corridor seemed to continue into the darkness. He turned around. He should have been able to see the glow of lights from the pool room radiating through the opaque glass doors, but only blackness loomed behind him. There seemed no alternative but to accept the anomaly. He shook out his tense limbs and kept moving forward.

Soon he noticed a faint glow ahead. A soft, constant flicker of orange light. He smelled sulfur and smoke and dampness in the air. It seemed that the corridor was gently curving. In a moment he saw that there were thick wax candles mounted on the walls. He stopped at the first one and examined it. Cylindrical white wax set in a cast-iron holder, its wick burned dim and there was no sign of melting. Brad raised his hand and felt no heat from the flame. Then he noticed that the wall itself had changed. The corridor was constructed from stone blocks. Brad could see the ancient chisel marks on each shaped stone. The passage had narrowed, claustrophobically, and continued to curve away lit by successive candles. At his feet Brad noticed the same marbled green asbestos tiles that floored the whole facility. They reflected the radiance of the candlelight on the curved space like dark mirrors.

Brad followed the arc forward. The walls moved closer until they were barely wider than his shoulders. He began to feel the closeness of the grave. His mind flashed with images of ancient crypts and lonely abandoned dungeons. Taunted by curiosity, he refused to let this haunting environment distract him or deter him. It wasn't courage that he felt, at least he didn't understand it in that way. It was the acceptance of a man doomed and bereft of choice.

Next, he saw something different ahead of him. The narrow passage seemed to come to an end further along. He could see faint natural light and for the first time in days, he felt the touch of fresh air on his face.

A black cast-iron gate barred the final arch of the stone passage and to Brad's relief it was unlocked and swung open with a rusty creak. He was outside. It was night. He stood in a garden. For the first time he could see the outer walls of St. Lucius, but to his surprise the facility was in front of him, across the expanse of the garden. The tunnel behind him opened from a slope on the edge of the forest.

A quarter moon drifting across the sky gave enough light that he could see the garden's breadth with unaided eyes. It occupied all the space between the forest and the facility. There was a flagstone path that issued from the tunnel behind him; it spread out like the branches of an old dead tree. Each narrow way was bordered by waist-high hedgerows and led to smaller tended plots, each acting as a hub to new paths in this botanical labyrinth. In the distance he saw dark walls where the hedges were much higher and where, he imagined, it would be easy to lose one's way in the maze. As he continued to scan the environment, he could see bright lights around an edge of the facility, and he guessed they were from the front entrance and the parking area he'd seen from his window. Turning back was useless. There was no telling where the tunnels' unnatural path might lead him next. Brad chose to move toward the light.

He found that the twisting path underfoot was filled with beauty, a stark contrast to the environs of St. Lucius. Even in the dim moonlight he could see the crisp trimming of the hedges. When he reached the hub gardens, he found them full of blooming flowers, open even in the night. There were stone benches and walled fountains flowing with clear water. The sweet smell of nectar filled his senses. He had never been one to appreciate the smell of flowers, but here the fresh fragrance was nothing short of rejuvenating. For a moment it took his mind away from the horrors that had been tormenting him. He walked slowly, enjoying the freedom of the outdoors. In random placement, pedestals poked from the shrubs holding statutes. Some held plump cherubs, while others were home to glaring snake-tailed gargoyles, still others had animals perched

- a lion, a wolf, a dolphin, even a dragon. Their forms were so realistic that their creators must surely have been masters of their art.

Distracted by these surroundings, Brad did not see a hidden obstacle at his feet. His foot caught on what felt like a branch or a root grown across the shadowed path beneath him. He fell forward scraping his palms on the flagstone. He cursed himself for his clumsiness and rolled over onto his seat. The short hedges around him created a long squat trench, and the moonlight overhead revealed the object of his fall. It appeared to be a root, thick, smooth, and pale in the glow. It reached entirely across the path. A short bulbus arch cleared the ground just high enough to catch a foot. Brad dusted his palms against each other before beginning to stand.

Somewhere close, he heard a sound. It was a loud clicking, rapid like a turning ratchet. Brad twisted his head. Whatever it was, it sounded right beside him through the short hedge. He froze, waiting to hear it again. Now he heard a different sound, like a heavy mallet dragged across stone. Near his outstretched legs he saw the root begin to move. The bulbus arch slowly bent upward revealing itself to be a joint. It slid sleepily across the path in front of him and further into the hedge. It was as thick as a human leg, the same pale color, but longer and hard shelled. The far extension of this limb came to a sharp fin-like point and was barbed with spines underneath. The pointed tip scraped across the flagstone as the entire appendage was withdrawn through the hedge wall. The rapid clicking sounded again right beside him.

Brad reacted. He flipped himself over and began to bound like an animal on all fours. He let out a cry. At that moment he heard a commotion in the bushes beside him.

Monster

Whatever this thing was, it seemed startled by his sudden movement and itself sprang to action. The sounds of clicking intensified, along with popping noises like the snapping of giant insect joints. Brad seemed to have set off a wave of activity throughout the garden. He pictured the panicked dispersal of the giant cave crickets he's witnessed from his window. This time he was the source of the pandemonium, and now he was caught among it. Something large leaped directly over his back. He did not see it, but he saw its shadow and felt its proximity. He had no doubt that these were the same creatures he had seen before, and he prayed that he could escape before they recovered from their startled state.

He came to another section of open garden. There was a statue and pedestal beside a bench. Brad crammed himself between them hiding. He dared not stand up for fear of being spotted or even inadvertently being pummeled by an enormous insect still in panicked flight leaping above the hedge-work. He waited there, knees clutched to his chest, imagining what shredding fate these creatures would convey upon him if he were caught. But after a few moments the sound of their fury slowed. Soon after, they nearly stopped. He had no confidence that the creatures had gone, but rather, he guessed that they had settled back into some nocturnal state of dormancy, one that had kept him from noticing them in the first place. He waited still listening. Soon again, it was quiet enough that he could relax his grip on his knees and refocus his thoughts.

Brad quietly crawled from his hiding space. The garden was as still as it had been before. Carefully, he raised himself to look around. It was the same garden, but now he was much closer to the building.

He could see it in greater detail now. It was primarily made of dark red brick and accented in carved stone block like he had seen in the tunnel. It was two-stories high with many windows; they stared back, dark, and empty as if it were itself alive and watching. A slate shingled roof reflected the moonlight.

In closest proximity was a single-story wing that reached out in his direction. Brad made sure that the garden around him remained quiet, then he started toward it with as much stealth as he could manage.

As he came nearer, he recognized where he was. He saw his own reflection in the glass of the approaching wing. He was outside of the pool room, and it was completely dark inside. There was no sign of Mal or any other member of the staff. Surely only enough time had passed to fish Ray's body from the pool. But would they have done it so quickly? Wouldn't they have at least made some show of an investigation? Or had Mal taken it upon himself to act alone? Brad had no idea what this all meant. Maybe he had just lost his sense of the passage of time. Maybe it was much later than he thought. Or maybe, he had imagined the entire incident and the darkness held no mystery at all.

Something rustled in bushes nearby.

Brad turned; his heart clutched in his chest. He imagined a giant insect moving toward him. It would emerge from the dark path between the high hedges and leap at him with its razor-sharp appendages. It would rip him apart and feed on his flesh. Perhaps this was his inevitable end. Perhaps it was the end he deserved.

The bushes swayed, and someone stepped into view. It was Mary.

She stopped suddenly and looked at him with wide awake eyes. She smiled when she recognized him. Brad smiled back, but his reaction was more one of relief. She wore her jeans and a pink, tight-fitting t-shirt. It had a decal of an adorable kitten across the front. Bold letters surrounded the cat, they read: *Love That Pussy.*

"Hi," Brad said, completely unprepared.

She seemed to scan him from head to toe, then back up his body. She continued to smile. Her long hair hung in her face, but Brad could see her eyes shining out at him. Her skin looked blemishless in the moonlight. "Couldn't sleep either, huh?"

Brad was tongue-tied. He was ragged from the intensity of the night. It had been a nightmare of murder, horrific creatures, and impossible realities. But it seemed that to Mary, it was no more than a case of insomnia. Something that a glass of warm milk might cure and make all go away. He faced her with silence.

Mary didn't wait for a response. She looked over at their reflection in the dark glass of the pool room, then back at him. "So, you killed Ray, huh?"

Brad's jaw dropped like lead. "How…?" was all he could muster.

"Oh, word gets around fast in this place," she said as casually as standing by a water cooler at break time. "Can't say I'm surprised, really. The way he was talking to you. All that craziness, like you were here just to cause him problems. If you ask me, the guy was an asshole. He deserved what he got."

Suddenly persuaded that his encounter with Ray was real, Brad did blame himself for his death. Killing him with his own hands was the only explanation that didn't require a supernatural intervention. But deep inside he must have felt differently. When caught off guard his response was defensive. "But I didn't," he said. "The water just opened up. I mean, and he was underneath. I tried to help, but…he drowned."

Mary casually examined his response. "So, you didn't kill him?" She squinted at him for a moment. "Huh," she said. "I believe that. You don't really strike me as a killer. It's not in your eyes. Usually, you can tell about these things, you know?"

Brad dropped his tense shoulders and let out a breath.

"You believe me?" he said.

"Sure, why not?" she answered. "You wouldn't lie to me, would you?"

"No, I guess not."

Brad's thoughts were spinning again. If he hadn't killed Ray, then the other things he'd seen must have been real. That couldn't be right. Maybe the truth was somewhere between. Maybe he was not a murderer, but he was still crazy.

Mary pulled a crumpled pack of cigarettes from her back pocket. She removed a cigarette and lit it with a match. The smell of sulfur was strong. "I want you."

"Excuse me?" Brad said.

"I said, do you want one?" she responded holding the pack out toward him.

"Oh," he replied. "No, no thanks. I don't smoke."

"Okay," she said. "I like to smoke when I come out here. The smoke keeps the bugs away."

He thought of the giant insects that had nearly torn him apart. He closed his eyes feeling pressure surge in his chest. There was no way that cigarette smoke would deter those horrible creatures. The idea strained credulity. He looked at her again. "You mean bugs, like mosquitoes and stuff?"

"No, I mean those giant fucking garden creatures. Those things are nasty. They don't mean to be, but they're big and jumpy, if you know what I mean. If you're not careful they'll tear you up. They're kind of touchy that way."

The surprises were coming in waves tonight. This one literally pushed him back. "You mean they're real?" he said. "I thought I was imagining things."

"Damn straight, they're real," she answered. "What did you think they were?"

"I don't know. I guess I thought I imagined them. I mean, I've never heard of anything like them. What are they?"

"Hell, if I know," Mary said releasing a lungful of smoke. "They're Gardeners. They come out at night, and they trim the hedges with their sharp legs. They feed on the scraps and pollinate the flowers. They're harmless unless you get in their way. You don't want to spook them or anything. I have no idea where they go in the daytime. Maybe into the forest, or maybe they burrow into the ground. I never paid that much attention. But, if you come out here at night, stay close to the building, and like I said, they don't like smoke."

"Oh my," said Brad, his mind nearing exhaustion. "This place is crazy. I can't believe what I'm seeing here. What is this place?"

Mary looked at him with an amused smile. She held her cigarette up close to her face. "You don't know, do you?" she asked, clearly surprised by the realization. "You really don't know?"

Brad's eyes lit up. "No," he said. "I don't know. Tell me... please. What is this place?"

Mary took a long slow drag from her cigarette. She seemed to be churning over a deliciously naughty thought. She scanned Brad again from head to toe. "I'll tell you what," she said. "Let's go up to my room and you can fuck me. And if you do good, then I'll tell you whatever you want to know." Her pretty smile broadened. "How's that for a deal?"

This time Brad was sure he'd heard her clearly. The abruptness made him flush and stirred some arousal. A sense of danger made the moment even more exciting. He looked at her tempting smile, her big alluring eyes. His own eyes dropped. It was obvious that she was not wearing a bra beneath her tight *Pussy* t-shirt. His gaze dropped further over her hips and stopped at her slender bare feet. He could imagine being with her. Their skin touching, beads of sweat lubricating their motion, the warmth of her body. He imagined closing his eyes and kissing her deeply, then lifting himself and looking into her face. What he saw was Sarah.

Like the opening of a parachute, jolting him back from freefall, the fantasy ripped away. The succubus spell was broken.

"No!" he said more assertively than he intended. "Sorry, but no... I'm married. I'm still trying to find my wife and my kid. I can't."

Mary looked at him and continued to smile. The denial seemed to have no effect on her. She blew out another cloud of smoke then crushed the cigarette butt out on the ground with her bare foot. She reached over and with a single finger traced the skin of his jawline.

"It's okay," she said. "I think that's sweet. But I'll be around if you change your mind."

"Yeah, sure," he said squirming at her touch. "I guess I better head back inside. Front door is this way, right?" he pointed over his shoulder.

"Just follow the path," she said. "And stay close to the building."

"Yeah, right," he said turning. "Thanks. Good night."

Brad walked away toward the light glowing around the edge of the building. In some way, he was pleased with himself, having declined Mary's offer, but he hated that his refusal had cost him the information he wanted so desperately. He'd have to find another way.

The path he followed made an angled turn along the outside of the pool wing and then hugged the edge of the brick wall. Brad kept his eyes peeled for the hideous Gardeners. He was in no mood for another chance encounter. When he reached the corner of the building he turned and looked back. If Mary was still there, then he couldn't see her in the darkness and shadows.

Beyond the corner, the outer grounds were well lit. Large spotlights mounted on the facility walls shined down upon the wide lawn that stretched its way toward the front entrance and the parking area. The lawn felt frighteningly exposed. There were many windows, including his own, that overlooked the area. Every one of them was dark, but each held potential eyes that seemed to track his movement.

He imagined that not everyone would be so trusting as to believe that he hadn't murdered Ray. And he certainly did not expect anyone to reward him with a proposition as friendly as the one made by Mary. But now he understood something. There was a bizarre reality about this place, where fantastic creatures roamed the gardens, and where the rules that he once thought governed nature were now no more than suggestions. He might still be losing his mind, but that no longer explained everything. There was a secret here. Mary seemed to know what it was, and maybe everyone else did too. Now, more than ever, Brad had to find the truth for himself.

Chapter Seven

It was two days before Jason's first birthday and unusually warm for that time of year. Sarah had taken Jason to visit with her parents. It was Jason's first trip on an airplane. Brad remembered seeing them both off at the airport terminal. He remembered kissing them good-bye outside of security and driving back home alone. He could have gone with them. Since Sarah's parents had paid for Sarah and Jason's tickets, Brad could have scrounged up enough money to pay for his own. But he knew better than to put himself through that torture. Her parents reviled him. He was under no illusion. Sure, they would have smiled and been on their best behavior, for Sarah's sake, but he knew the score. He always had. He was nothing but a heathen in their eyes, the blasphemous bastard that had knocked up their only daughter.

Sarah promised she would be back on the morning of Jason's birthday and Brad already had plans to pick them up when they arrived. It was better that he stayed home. Sarah and

Christopher Cunningham

Jason could enjoy their time away spent with family, and Brad could continue to work to support his family.

Brad hated his job. He was 2nd Assistant Manager at the *Buy-4-Less* grocery store. This was the culmination of six years of under-paid, non-challenging drudgework that he called a profession. The store manager, Paul, was only a little older than Brad, and he still lived at home with his mother. Brad would have to push him in front of a truck before Brad got a shot at the top position. Even then, he'd have to deal with the 1st Assistant Manager, Bennie. That bloated pig would probably die of a heart attack or diabetes before he hit thirty. If Brad wanted his job, he would only have to feed his steady supply of snack cakes and pork rinds.

The only thing that made work bearable was that there were a couple of good-looking young girls who worked as cashiers. Tracie and Valerie were their names. They were both over eighteen years old, dumb as a bag of rocks, and hot enough to grace a magazine cover. They both went through boyfriends like bubblegum, discarding them once they'd sucked out the flavor. But even so, Brad always got the vibe that they thought he was cool. At twenty-seven, he was an older guy, but not creepy old. He was relatively good looking, and he wore a ring where a wedding ring was usually worn. It was a simple gold band that made him seem off-limits. It made him feel good, to imagine at least, that they saw him as sexy and attractive. But the reality was, for all intents and purposes, he was unofficially married to Sarah, and he never once acted upon his fantasies.

It was a Tuesday night. He'd had the day off. He was supposed to be off every Tuesday and Thursday, but that almost never happened. Brad was always working shifts for cashiers and stock boys that didn't show up for work. This week it was his only day off. He traded a shift with Bennie so that he could take Sarah and Jason to the airport. Later, it would be the same since he'd need to pick them up too. Now that evening rolled around, he sat on his couch, eating cold pizza, and watching one of his favorite movies on disk, a remastered copy of *The Toxic Avenger*.

The doorbell rang.

Brad sat up and looked around. Blood rushed to his face. No one came to visit him unannounced. He didn't really have any friends. The pizza had arrived without incident over an hour ago and he wasn't expecting any other deliveries. He paused his movie and stood up.

For some reason he turned and looked at the living room window. It was dark outside, and he could see nothing but his own reflection and that of the room around him. They lived in a crappy little one-bedroom apartment in a non-descript part of town. It was a ground floor unit with no sliding glass door or patio. That had been a pricey up-grade they had decided to forgo. He wasn't sure why he looked in the opposite direction from the front door.

The bell rang again.

He put down the remote control and walked to the front door only a few feet away. Brad leaned into the door and put his eye to the peephole. The fish-eyed lens revealed Valerie, one of his young cashiers. She was looking around, nervously biting her lip. Brad's heart immediately began beating hard in his chest. He couldn't for the life of him imagine what she was doing there. She wouldn't have come to his home if there were a problem at work.

Just as she seemed about to walk away, Brad slid the chain on his side of the door. The sound spun her attention back to her unknown purpose. Brad cracked it open and looked out at her.

"Hi," she said with a pretty smile. She wore a winter coat and a knit cap on her head. She swayed back and forth, shifting her weight on the balls of her feet.

"Hi, Val," Brad answered looking down on her small frame. "Is everything alright?"

"Oh yeah," she said. "I was just around, you know. I remember you saying that you lived here."

"Yeah?" he nodded.

"Yeah." She swiveled her upper body on her hips. "I heard Bennie say that your family was out of town. I thought maybe I'd stop by and say hi. See what you were up to. You know."

"Yeah, um, I was just watching a movie," he said. His heart was still pounding. Heat rose from the skin of his face.

"Oh yeah, what are you watching?"

"Just a dumb horror movie," he answered. "You wouldn't be interested, I'm sure."

"Oh," she said. She looked around again. "Can I come in? It's kind of cold out here." Now she looked directly up into his eyes. Hers were big and round with long lashes. She never wore this much make-up at work.

Brad looked back and forth down the apartment buildings hallway. It was well lit and comfortable. He was wearing a t-shirt. "Yeah, I guess."

He stepped back, opening the door wide. Valerie moved, brushing past him and was in his living room. Brad closed the door and watched her as she slowly meandered. She took off her hat and shoved it in her coat pocket. With her back to him she shook out her hair and ran her fingers through it, refreshing its curl. She looked around at the pictures on the walls, the photos on tabletops and on a bookshelf; there was a playpen in the corner. She slowly let her coat drop off her shoulders then hung it over her arm. She spun back around facing him.

"I like your place," she smiled.

She looked gorgeous.

"Thanks," he said. Stepping passed her he grabbed the remote from the coffee table and turned off the T.V. dispelling the frozen image of the Toxic Avenger hurling a 50-gallon barrel of radio-active waste. "You want a slice of pizza? It's kind of cold, but I can throw it in the microwave if you want?"

"No thanks," she said. "Do you have anything to drink? A beer or something?"

"Um, yeah. Out in the fridge. Hold on a sec." Brad turned quickly and stepped into the kitchen. He couldn't believe this was happening. It was so out of the blue. He grabbed a beer from the refrigerator and stepped back into the living room.

Val was sitting on the couch now. He handed her the beer. She smiled at him.

"Listen, I need to use the bathroom. I'll be right back," he said.

"Okay."

Brad slipped into the short hall and closed the bathroom door behind him. He leaned on the sink and stared at himself in the mirror. He sucked in a deep breath and released it. His heart was still pounding. There was a beautiful girl drinking beer out on his couch. He thought he'd sensed a vibe from her before, but he never imagined she would act on it. This was the kind of thing that only existed in the minds of teenaged boys. What was she thinking, he wondered? She knew he was married, and she knew his wife was out of town. He tried for an instant to believe this was just as she portrayed, a friendly visit with a co-worker, but that was ridiculous. He knew why she was here. He could feel the sexual tension. The pheromones were so thick that he was already at half-mast. He untucked his t-shirt to try and cover his reaction. This was so uncool. He understood that completely. This was not just some adolescent fantasy. There was a real, live, hot chick right outside his door. All he had to do was…

Then he thought about Sarah. He could see her face as plain as his own in the mirror. He could see the long, thin silver cross that she always wore around her neck. How could he do this to her? How could he even think about it?

Of course, he hadn't done anything. He didn't invite Val over. As far as he could remember, he never said or did anything openly to send the message that he would be interested. She was just one of those hot chicks that got what she wanted. She'd flash a smile and a little skin and guys would roll over for her. But Brad wasn't like them, he was a married man, a father.

But that wasn't true, was it? He and Sarah weren't married. And that wasn't his fault. That was her decision. And fatherhood? Well, that was her choice too. If it had been up to him…

Damn, why was this happening? He couldn't tell if his pounding heart were from lust, or the crushing guilt that was his constant companion. Either way he felt like shit now. He was almost sick to his stomach.

That's it, he thought, it wasn't worth it. If the guilt were this powerful now, then what would it be like if he followed through with this girl? He took a moment to breathe again. He made up his mind. He would go back out, sit down, and let her finish her beer. Then he would politely send her on her way. He might knock down her confidence a notch, but he would prove that he was a nice guy, the mature one, and in the end, would probably come across even more attractive for denying her. After all, people always wanted what they couldn't have. This whole situation was a case in point.

He opened the door and stepped back into the living room.

Val was no longer on the couch. There was no way he could have missed her in the small room. He popped his head into the kitchen beside him and found it empty as well.

"Hey Val?" he called.

"Back here."

Her voice came from the bedroom.

He turned, passed the bathroom, and stood in the doorway of the room he shared with Sarah. There was a queen-sized bed, two dressers, nightstands, a laundry basket, and an empty crib beside the only window. Val sat on the bed; her coat laid out beside her. Her beer sat sweating and unopen on the nightstand. She was wearing a blouse with buttons down the front. They were halfway undone. In profile Brad could see the slope of her bra and half of her young breast. His penis jumped with an uncontrolled twitch.

"Hey, ummm," was all he could say.

"Come here," she said in a voice that seemed practiced.

Brad stepped forward without thinking. His brain pumped with chemicals. She stood up and put her hands on his upper arms. She pressed her body against him.

"You seem nervous. Are you okay?" she asked.

"Ah, well, listen…" he managed.

She slowly dropped a hand and pressed it firmly against the front of his pants. "Mmmmm," she purred.

Brad practically swooned. His blood flowed quickly in response. He started to lean forward with his face toward hers. She looked up and angled toward him.

Then a noise came from the living room. A door opened and let in a mind-sheering scream. It was the baby; it was Jason. And that could only mean that Sarah was here, home early from her trip.

"Hey sweetie, I'm home!" she shouted over the baby's crying.

The realization struck Brad like a lightning bolt. This was it. He was fucked, and not in a good way. He spun out of Val's embrace so fast that it knocked her back toward the bed. He swung the bedroom door closed, the last millimeters in slow motion to keep the latch from clicking too loud. He pushed the button lock on the doorknob.

"Fuck, you've got to get out of here!" he shouted in a whisper to Val.

Val looked at him with clear irritation. "Jesus Christ, what's wrong with you?" she said at normal volume. She began to slowly re-button her shirt.

Brad didn't know what to say. Val didn't seem to get what was going on here. Maybe she just didn't care.

Luckily, Jason's screaming from the living room masked whatever noise they were making. But Brad understood that his life as he knew it was in free-fall, like the final grains in a cracked hourglass.

"Brad! Are you here?" Sarah's voice raised from outside.

"I'll be out in a second!" he shouted back.

He rushed to the window and threw open the sash. "Come on!" he said to Val. "You've got to go. That's my wife."

"I thought she wasn't coming back until later," she said.

"I don't fucking know, but she's here! You need to get out of here!" he pleaded.

"I'm not climbing through a window," she said. "You'll just have to deal with this."

Jason's screaming became louder. The locked doorknob rattled, then three hard knocks came on the bedroom door. "Baby, are you alright in there?" Sarah was standing right on the other side.

Brad stood wide-eyed and shaking. He struggled to think rationally. He already felt caught. His life as he knew it was over, all in a split second. Cold sweat broke from his pours, down his forehead, soaking his collar. A pressure built deep in his gut as if some creature stirred in his stomach, blindly trying to escape the boiling cauldron of acid there.

He snatched up Val's coat from the bed and tossed it out the window. "Get the fuck out!" he said in the loudest voice he could get away with.

Val returned a look of indignation. "Fuck you."

Brad grabbed her arm and dragged her to the window. This fucking bitch was going to ruin his life. And she didn't even fucking care. He could see her smug look. It made him want to punch her right in her self-righteous face.

"Get out the fucking window or you're fired," he threatened.

Apparently, no had ever spoken to her that way before. Insult was written on her every fiber. "You're an asshole, you know that?" she said. "I swear, you're going to be sorry for this." Finally, she relented. She turned and began to climb through.

Brad bounced on the balls of his feet, willing her to go faster. He gave her a little lift and shove.

Once she was through and standing on the grass outside, she turned her face back to him. "You're going to be sorry, asshole."

Brad had no time to even consider her threat. He closed the window and turned the latch.

Jason's screaming was more distant now, but more brisk knocks came to the bedroom door. Brad quickly ripped back the bedspread and sheets, ruffled his pillow, then bounded to the door. He opened it slowly and saw Sarah standing right in front of him. She looked up at him and her face immediately changed to an expression of concern.

"Oh my," she said. "You look awful, are you alright?" She reached up and smoothed the hair from his brow. "My goodness, you're so pale and clammy. Are you coming down with something?"

Brad was still shaking. "Yeah, sorry. I'm not feeling so good. I think it was the pizza. I was just trying to sleep it off. That's why it took so long to open the door. I thought I was dreaming that you came home."

"Oh, you poor thing," she said. Sarah took his hand and led him back to the bed. She urged him to lay down. Then she noticed the beer on the nightstand. "What's this?"

Brad had forgotten all about it. His stomach twisted, then he thought of a new lie. "It was cold. I was using it like an ice pack on my forehead. It felt good."

Sarah touched the sweaty can. "Well, it's not cold anymore. Let me get you a washcloth. I'll soak it in cold water."

Brad smiled up at her. "Thanks."

"Let me get Jason settled first," she said. "I'll keep him in the playpen tonight. Let you get some rest. It's been a long day for all of us."

Brad touched her arm. "What happened? Why are you back so early? Is everything alright?"

"Mom wasn't feeling well either. I think she's coming down with the flu or something. I thought it was best to bring Jason home so that he didn't get sick too. Not with his first birthday coming up." She patted Brad's hand. "I guess I should have called, but I thought it would be a nice surprise. We took an Uber from the airport. Oh well, damned if I do, damned if I don't…You just relax sweetheart. I'll be back in a few minutes…Love you."

"Love you, too," he smiled as she turned and left the room.

Brad let out an enormous breath. His muscles ached from the tension. The sweat on his skin made him feel cold. He could taste bile in his mouth. But more than anything, there was a horrible pressure on his chest, like some heavy weight sat there, sucking out his breath and his energy. It was the weight of guilt, his invisible demon familiar. One that continued to grow, day by day. One that he could not avoid feeding. He hated it, and he hated himself for letting it thrive within him.

Christopher Cunningham

This was the worst night of his life, he thought. He had never been so frightened of losing everything he cared about, the only things that were important to him. Looking back, there was no way he could have imagined that things would get worse. Maybe he'd just been a fool not to see it, blind to the inevitable. But one thing was certain. It was his fault, and he would have to bear the guilt for everything that came after.

Chapter Eight

Brad sat on the broad steps of St. Lucius Sanitarium. Above him spanned the high arch of the outer foyer. The cut stones of its construction balanced, leaning one against the next. The center headstone had a carving of the ever-seeing eye. The empty parking lot of neatly raked fine gravel centered before him and the stair, and gave origin to the narrow road that passed into the dark forest beyond. Even the passing footprints of Brad's walk across the gravel were no longer visible, swallowed somehow, like tracks on wind-swept desert dunes.

Brad waited to go back inside because he had not yet decided what he was supposed to do. He leaned forward, elbows upon his knees, and grasped his head with his scraped hands. His skull ached like a swelling balloon. His encounter with Mary had brought back painful memories, and he'd fought the temptation to accept her primal offer. She held an attraction that he hadn't felt for Sarah in a long time, but he knew it was only physical. He knew more than most how wrong that attraction was, and the guilt it would fester. But he wanted so badly to know about this God forsaken place. Was he going insane or was this place itself a manifestation of madness? It held some secret, one he yearned to understand. But at what cost? What promises would he have to betray? What love must he abandon? What was he willing to live with?

He stood up, stepped across the foyer, and went through the front doors.

The single light on the reception desk made it appear like a set piece under a spotlight on a dark stage. It barely illuminated the tiled columns that stood like waiting ghosts in the wings. Sister Kayla was there, now returned to her mark. She sat, head tilted down, reading a book under the green shaded lamp. Kayla looked up at him with a smile as he approached. There was no sign of surprise on her pretty young face, as if he were right on queue.

"Hello, Mr. Turner. Out getting some air?" she said in her mousey voice.

"You could say that," he answered. He had almost forgotten his earlier impression of her, but it renewed immediately meeting her again. There was something sweet and pure about her manner and lovely appearance. She was tiny in stature and seemed more so with her black habit blending with the darkness behind her. The skin of her face was soft and pale, her eyes wide and bright, her smile genuine as truth incarnate. Just being in her presence improved his mood.

"Is there anything that I can help you with?" she asked.

"Not unless you can give me a ride home," he said half joking.

She practically giggled. It was a reminder that joy was still alive in a world corrupted.

"Oh, Mr. Turner. I wish I could."

"I believe you," he responded.

"Are you off to bed?"

"I don't know. I don't think I could sleep if I did."

She nodded her head almost imperceptibly. "Mr. Sharpe was asking about you. He went down the corridor looking for you not ten minutes ago. I'm not sure where he's gotten off to now though."

"Mr. Sharpe?" he tilted his head. "Oh yeah, Antony," he made the connection. He shook his head slowly. "I'm not sure how much more I can take for one night."

Kayla looked up at him with a tender smile. She started to say something, then stopped herself. She looked left and right, as if to confirm that they were alone. Then she leaned forward and whispered. "Don't worry about Mr. Raymond," she said. "It's alright." She raised a finger to her lips and shushed.

Brad took a step back. What did she mean by that? Obviously, she must have known about what happened. He wanted to question her, but he felt an obligation to respect her signal of silence. It was clear she was breaking some rule by even mentioning the subject.

Now he was sure he would not be able to sleep. He would lay in bed for hours mulling over everything that pinballed through his brain. He needed to continue to look for answers. He slipped his hands into his pockets and felt the small flashlight that he had taken from Sister Kayla's desk. He pulled it out.

"Oh, I'm afraid I borrowed your flashlight without asking." He handed it out for her.

Sister Kayla continued her secretive whisper. "You hold on to that for now," she said. "You might need it. You can return it when you're done."

"Thank you," he smiled.

Brad slipped it back into his pocket and began to turn away. As he did, he caught a glimpse of the book she was reading. She held it absently half open. The pages were blank. "Good night," he said to her.

"Good night, Mr. Turner."

He left the light of her desk and walked toward the shadowy corridor. The hallway was unchanged as he entered. Darkness pressed against him like a thick fog, isolating, but he could still make out his reflection following in the floor beneath his feet. He came again to the intersection of the basement alcove, the pool wing, and the unexplored corridor. He couldn't explain how he'd gotten lost earlier in the night. There was no sign of the narrow stone tunnel that led to the garden. But for now, he felt certain that this was the corridor he had planned to explore. After a brief pause, he went forward fully aware that reality and rationality were no longer constants that he could rely on.

This new passage was surprisingly *unsurprising*. It did not turn into a stone tunnel; it did not become the stinking, living bowel of a hideous giant; it did not lead to some alien dimension, at least not in a way that was obvious to him. It probed straight on, dark doorways punctuating the walls, exposed pipes and conduits hiding in the spaces where the ceiling tiles were no more, clumps of plaster fallen to the shiny polished floor from their former grip on exposed wood lathe.

Monster

The only thing that surprised him was that his night vision was improved. He could see these details now, where before the darkness had been near complete. He did not question this turn of good favor, but he held tight to the knowledge that he had a working flashlight in his pocket.

As he continued forward his mind began to wander. The search for Antony's boy brought him back to his childhood friend, Tommy Perkins. He had to wonder what had ever happened to Tommy. He wondered if his scars had ever healed. Was he out there somewhere with a wife and children of his own? Was he happy? Had he been able to leave his past behind or was he haunted and tormented too? Brad hadn't thought about that day in years. He wasn't sure if he'd blocked it out intentionally or not. But right now, those memories came flooding back into his conscious and he could see it all with perfect clarity.

It was the Friday after Thanksgiving. It was cold and the smell of woodsmoke lay strong across the neighborhood. Most of the leaves had already fallen and many of the lawns were spotted in brown, red, yellow, and orange. The colors swished and crunched under his feet. He kicked at them with his long strides and left a trail of tossed leaves in his wake. He was on his way over to Tommy's house.

He hadn't seen him the day before due to the holiday. Brad and his parents, along with his grandmother, had shared their traditional turkey dinner. Besides Christmas, this was Brad's favorite holiday. The whole house filled with the smell of the roasting turkey and all the fixings that went with it. The mouth-watering anticipation as his father carved at the table. They were memories of childhood that he would never forget.

Tommy, on the other hand, had no such expectation that year. His mother and father had split up the month before. Tommy's father packed most of his things and left. Soon afterward, Tommy's Uncle Mike moved in with them, and Thanksgiving was not on the agenda. Tommy said his mother had been sick. She was spending all her time locked in her bedroom. At night, he told Brad, he would lay in bed and listen to her cry until he finally fell asleep.

Brad understood at some level how terrible this was for Tommy; it made him wonder what it would be like to lose one of his own parents. But Brad had suffered no tragedy in his own life, no loss that compared to Tommy's. At eleven years old, Brad couldn't possibly fathom the deep pain of the separation or how it tore his friend apart.

Now that the holiday was behind them, Brad went to see Tommy as if it were any other evening.

Brad took a shortcut through a neighbor's property, climbed a short fence, and approached Tommy's place through his backyard. It was early evening, and the sky above was a fading gray. Most of the neighboring houses were lit by orange windows against an orange sunset horizon. By contrast, Tommy's house was dark. As Brad walked beside it, a basement window threw out the only sign of life, trembling light from the window well. Curious, Brad knelt on the ground and peered inside.

He was looking into their finished basement. It was set up as a family room. Golden oak paneling and bookshelves lined the walls, along with family photos. A ping-pong table sat near the steps that came down from above. Tommy's dad had not yet collected his sports memorabilia. Autographed baseballs lined a shelf and several bats hung in a rack next to framed posters of stadiums and sports teams. Shaded lamps around the room gave everything a fiery glow. On a brown upholstered couch Tommy sat with his Uncle Mike. Their backs were to the window. Uncle Mike was wearing the black priest shirt he always wore, and oddly, Tommy's shoulders were bare. They were watching television. Brad could tell from the picture quality that they were watching a well-worn video tape.

Brad looked at the T.V. and was initially confused. Swirling flesh-tones moved back and forth in close-up. Then the camera view changed, and Brad suddenly realized that there was a group of naked people, touching each other, kissing each other's bodies, rubbing against each other. Tommy and his Uncle Mike were watching a dirty movie.

Brad knew what a dirty movie was. He'd heard other kids joke about them, but he'd never seen one. A sickening sensation moved through him, and his body reacted. His stomach bunched into knots and his heart began to race. Leaning forward on his hands and knees his limbs became wobbly. Brad knew what sex was. He knew where babies came from. But what he witnessed was not natural. It wasn't about making babies. He couldn't really fathom why this was wrong, but his physical reaction confirmed it. The body parts looked alien and frightfully strange. Nothing like his own eleven-year-old body or his imaginings about girls his age. Like a horror show, he wanted to turn away, but he could not. Then the thought of being caught took hold of him. He almost retched, but still, he couldn't pull himself away.

Then he saw Tommy and Uncle Mike swing their heads. But it wasn't Brad they were reacting to. Uncle Mike jumped up. His pants were around his ankles, and he struggled to pull them up quickly without losing his balance. Standing at the bottom of the steps, frozen, was Tommy's mom. Brad heard her scream at Uncle Mike. How Brad could have ever forgotten that look on her face, the disgust, the hate, and her sudden turn to anger, he could never explain. Even the memory of it spiked his blood pressure.

Tommy jumped up from the couch and ran to his mother. He showed no sign of modesty as he stood stripped naked and sheltering behind her. Brad couldn't begin to describe his emotions. His friend looked so young. This couldn't possibly have been the same kid that was his friend, the one who he played with and laughed with and dreamed with. Brad watched this all with a wave of heat washing across his red face, as Tommy stood pale and blank like a disconnected robot child.

Uncle Mike turned off the television and stood with gesturing hands. His black priest shirt hung untucked, his white collar loose around his neck. He seemed to be pleading with Tommy's mom. He dropped to his knees begging with clasped hands. But Tommy's mom was having none of it. Brad could feel her wrath filling the room; her eyes took on a murderous rage.

In an almost graceful motion, Tommy's mom grabbed a baseball bat from the rack beside her. She took a few quick steps forward and swung it at Uncle Mike. He went down. Tommy's mom stepped forward again. Still screaming, she raised the bat over her shoulder.

Brad clamped his eyes. He practically collapsed away from the window. Brad jumped to his feet and ran home as fast as he could, his heart racing and his legs stinging with speed.

Brad never told anyone about what he witnessed. He spent the rest of the holiday weekend in bed. He told his parent he didn't feel well, and that was the truth. Brad never learned the details of what happened that night, though the incident seemed to be big news in the neighborhood. Brad's parents had little to say to him about it. He understood that they wanted to shelter him. But there was no shelter from the images that seemed poised to last forever.

Still, those memories were not what affected him most. They were not the worst thing to come from that night.

Tommy never returned to school again after that. Their house went quickly up for sale. The day that they moved away Tommy came to Brad's house to say good-bye to his best friend. But Brad asked his mother to send him away. Only in looking back on it now did he realize that he couldn't confront his own feelings. He didn't understand them. He had no idea what to say to his friend. He just wanted to run away and never think of that night again.

Brad stood hidden behind a curtain at the front window of his house and looked out at Tommy. It was the last time he would ever see him. And that look on Tommy's face burned into his brain. Only later would he understand how completely he had abandoned his friend, and how that betrayal added to the torment that Tommy must have felt. Brad denied him the one moment when his friendship would have meant the most. Instead, he abandoned their friendship to die. That look on Tommy's face, the one that Brad had tried so hard to forget, had arisen again on the face of Antony's son.

With that awful image lingering in his mind, Brad was suddenly distracted by something new. From somewhere ahead in the dim, crumbling hallway he heard a soft voice, a child's voice. Was it Tommy's voice? Of course not, Brad dismissed. It was coming from the next dark doorway to his right. But he recognized the words. He knew them from his own childhood. Though now they brought different images to mind than he imagined as a child.

> "Now I lay me down to sleep.
> I pray the Lord my soul to keep.
> If I should die before I wake.
> I pray the Lord my soul will take."

An ice-cold chill ran down Brad's spine. Even for someone like Brad, who did not hold any real religious belief, these words were etched upon his psyche. He'd never really thought about them. Not until now. This was a cute little children's rhyme. One his grandmother had whispered to him at bedtime. But hearing it in the present context, it made him cringe. He imagined a poor child, praying in the dead of night for their eternal soul, and entrusting that soul to a magical being with the power to save and give life. Then, accepting that death was more than mere possibility, and with redemption unlikely, committing their soul to the very being who'd abandoned them. It sounded like the terrible climax of one of the horror movies that he once loved. And most appalling of all, Brad had recited this to his own son, never stopping to examine its meaning. Thankfully, Jason was too young to understand the words.

Brad's nerves were tight. He forced himself to approach the dark doorway from where the voice had come. Peering inside he saw what appeared to be a playroom. There were under-sized tables and chairs, shelves with discarded toys and story books. A rug with woven roads and buildings for toy cars to roam. It was what anyone might imagine finding in a children's ward of a hospital or a daycare. But this room seemed long abandoned. Chairs were fallen over, toys strewn dusty on the floor and in corners, children's posters hung half torn from the walls. A bank of frosted windows shined with a hint of moonlight over the dim space.

Among the jumble Brad saw what he was looking for. Sitting on the rug near the center of the room was the boy he had seen at the therapy session, the boy he knew to be Antony's son. The boy was backlit from the glowing windows, his face in shadow. He wore the same jeans and tennis shoes as before, and the black hoody pulled over his head like the grim reaper, the front zipper was closed tight to warn off the cold damp air.

Brad cleared his voice primarily to alert the boy of his presence, but also to confirm to himself that this figure was real and not a dream. He took a few very slow steps into the room. In his pocket he held onto the flashlight, but he did not light it. The boy was looking down at the floor in front of his crossed legs. He had two G.I. Joe dolls, action figures dressed in fatigues. One he held standing beside his knee, the other lay on its' back. Brad had the impression that the standing doll was the one the boy spoke through when he'd recited the prayer, the prone doll was the apparent soulless recipient. Brad continued his cautious approach until he was right in front of the boy. Finally, he knelt across from him.

"Hi there. My name's Brad, what's yours'?"

The boy did not respond, he didn't look up.

"What do you got there?" Brad continued. "Those are G.I. Joe's, right? I used to have a collection of them when I was a kid. They're pretty cool. I used to have all kinds of adventures with mine. What are yours' up to?"

The kid sat quiet; he still held the one doll upright. He did not meet Brad's eyes. Finally, he spoke in a muffled voice. "It's a funeral," he said.

That was the last thing Brad expected to hear, but under the circumstances he shouldn't have been surprised, he thought. Still, it made the encounter even stranger than it had begun. It made the darkness seem darker.

"Oh, I'm sorry," seemed to be the appropriate thing for Brad to say. He didn't want to know the details. "What's your name, son?" he asked leaning slightly forward.

"Todd," the boy answered slowly. "Todd Sharpe."

"Your dad's name is Antony, right? I know your dad. He says he's really worried about you. He's afraid something bad happened to you and that you might be hurt."

Still the boy did not move or look up at Brad.

"Can I tell him that you're alright? How about you come with me and we can show him that you're alright? I know he'll be happy to see you."

Brad sat on his haunches waiting for Todd to respond. Maybe this was the wrong approach, he thought. Obviously, Antony had not killed his son, but he may still have hurt him. Antony was in this place for a reason, and child abuse would surely fit the criteria. Todd might have good reason to fear his father. Brad decided to change his line of questions to what really concerned him.

"Todd, I'm guessing you've been here for some time, on your own maybe, in this place. I'm wondering, are there other people like you? I mean, people who are living here that are hiding, or maybe being hidden from the rest?"

There was no reaction.

"Todd, I'm asking because I'm looking for someone. My family. I have a wife named Sarah and a little boy named Jason. Jason's just a baby, just one year old. Have you seen anyone like that? Have you seen my family?"

Still no response.

Brad leaned forward. "Todd?" He placed his hand on the boy's shoulder and was pulled by a sudden force and swirl of disorientation.

Brad fell forward like being sucked into a blackhole in outer space. All things of light and matter were left behind him and beyond an invisible event horizon. A twisting wormhole of stretching black plasma sped by at speeds beyond comprehension. The sensation of falling was strong, but soon changed as if he were holding still and this dark region of reality sped past him. He stopped so suddenly that he felt his guts slosh against his ribs.

Brad was now standing in a ruined building. Black charred timbers and half collapsed walls gave form to its former purpose. It was a church. Whatever fire that consumed this place had come and gone long ago. The crushed pews were tumbled and rotted from exposure, as were the remaining walls and woodwork. The ceiling was ripped away, and Brad could see dark gray storm clouds rushing overhead. Faded and smeared bible pages blew haphazard through the whipping air. Between the spaces where windows used to be, he could see the skeletons of winter trees swaying in the strong winds of a coming tempest. The barometric pressure was changing drastically and pressing painfully against his ears. This surreal place was stinging cold and frighteningly loud.

High above him he saw the stone frame of a bell tower. It leaned dangerously toward him, ready to collapse and demolish what remained intact below. But still the iron bell hung there. It swayed slowly and reluctantly in the growing gale. Its faint tolling was a sad din of foreboding. If there had been an empty tomb open before him, he would gladly have crawled inside and sought refuge from the oppression he felt weighing on him. He struggled with the allure of escape through suicide.

Then he saw that he was not alone. Two figures crouched on the ground, surrounded by debris, and sheltering beneath the black charred alter.

Brad wrapped his arms around himself, hunching his shoulders to fend off the cold wind. He stumbled forward through the ruin trying to avoid broken glass and rusty nails, and spearheads of splintered wood. He could hear desperate shouting by one of the figures. Then he recognized them. It was Antony squatting on the ground; he held his son tightly to his chest with one arm. With his other arm he held a fist shaking defiantly at the raging storm. He was shouting over the driving wind, fuming in rebellion.

"I won't do it!" he shouted at the sky. "I can't! Take me, please take me instead! I'm begging you!"

"Antony!" Brad shouted at him. "Antony, come on! We need to get to shelter!"

Brad moved closer but realized that Antony was not aware of his presence there. He saw Todd's face pressed against his father's chest. The boy looked up at his father, eyes round and staring. Then Todd's eyes shifted; they looked up at the sky above. Todd's lips peeled away from his gritted teeth. His eyes now bulged from their sockets. The look Brad saw on the boy's face passed to him like a contagion as his own heart raced and pounded.

Monster

Then Brad heard it. It may have been the loudest thing he had ever heard, like a fleet of cargo ships blasting their horns at once. Brad had to duck and clamp his hands to his ears. He spun around following the boy's gaze over his shoulder at the sky. Something vast dipped down through the dense charcoal cloud cover. A great ribbed belly of gray flesh hundreds of feet above. The Leviathan swam there. It rolled to its side, pushing down an enormous fin, fanning the clouds and whipping tornadoes to life in its wake. Brad realized that most of its bulk was unseen above the clouds. He wasn't sure his sanity would survive beholding its entirety. As it passed overhead its hind section came into partial view. Brad expected to see some giant fantail fluke like that of a whale, instead it split into dozens of tentacles, hundreds of yards long, fluttering slowly behind it as if flowing through deep dark water.

But the appearance of this thing was not what struck him most. It was a sensation of presence that it conveyed. It vibrated deep inside of him, a confrontation with indestructible power, so vast and strong that it need only think of him in passing and he would be utterly destroyed. But he also recognized an ambiguity of mind, a complete void of compassion. He had no other sense of its intent, only of his own insignificance. He felt like a matchbook on the face of the sun.

Brad crouched among the debris, hiding for the sake of instinct rather than some hope of safety. He cowered as he watched the great Leviathan roll into the distance and sail back up into the storm clouds. Brad stayed motionless, fighting to regain his senses and the courage to move again. Finally, he looked around him. Through the ruined walls of the church, he saw a wild pack of screaming tornadoes left in the wake of the

Leviathan's passing. They roamed the surrounding horizon, ripping trees from the earth and tossing them like twigs high into the atmosphere. Once again, Brad's instincts cried for shelter.

He got up from the ground crouching. A few feet away he saw Antony still holding tight to his son. Brad made his way toward them.

"Antony! Come on, we have to go!" he shouted over the tumult.

Antony did not respond, and Brad remembered that he did not seem to see him there.

Antony looked down at Todd in his arms. "I'm so sorry son! You saw it, you know what it is! I can't fight it! You understand, don't you? Please say you understand!"

Todd returned his father's gaze. The boy looked exhausted, spent of energy. He made no sign of response.

The wind screamed around them. A tornado rampaged in the nearby forest throwing debris dangerously close. Brad hunkered down in front of his oblivious companions. He watched as Antony reached into his open jacket and retrieved a long, curved blade. He pulled Todd away from his clutch and exposed his unguarded chest.

"I'm so sorry!" he shouted. Antony raised the knife.

Brad reacted. He threw himself forward and put his hands on Antony's shoulder, blocking the downward strike.

In that instant, Brad was falling again, ripped and swirling in a tremendous vortex. At first, he believed that he had been snatched up into a tornado and was an instant from being torn apart, but then he realized he was once again in the black wormhole that had brought him into this nightmare. Now, he surrendered to it. He had little energy left to fight or struggle. The experience lasted for only a few moments, then he felt the inertia suddenly stop and was slammed back into a static world.

He pulled his hand back from where it rested on Todd's shoulder like jerking back from a hot stove. Brad's head was spinning. He tried to grasp whether the experience he'd just had were real, or if it were some hallucination. Surely, he had to hope for hallucination; that was clearly the default position. Flying through vortices in time and space was entirely outside the realm of science as he understood it. And he had already decided that the Leviathan was a mere symbol of his own feelings of helplessness. He was suffering from textbook psychosis. The stress of losing his family, the frightening search for Antony's son, they had brought it on. And the only cure was finding his family and getting the hell out of this place. He still believed that young Todd might be the key. He might still have the answers he was looking for. And here he was, alive and well in the real world. Brad forced himself to focus.

Todd sat across from him, his face in the shadow of his hoodie. Slowly he raised his head so that Brad could see him. He no longer wore the face of sadness or innocence. He slowly broke into a smile, and it seemed like a smile of cold pride. It was the smile he might expect to see on an adult Tommy Perkins, an accusing smile. An avenging smile.

Todd let go of the G.I. Joe still held upright in his hand. The doll leapt into a stance of panic, then ran swiftly into the darkness around them under its own power. It squealed, like an evading rat. It disappeared into the dark scatter of loose toys and abandoned playroom furniture.

Brad fell back from his haunches onto his butt with a gasp. His eyes scanned for the tiny, animated figure, watching for it to reappear and pounce. He looked back at Todd. The boys' gaze never faltered. He continued to stare and smile. Brad fumbled the flashlight out of his pocket. He turned it on to scan the room for the doll that now controlled his attention. The beam fell on the other doll first, the one that had been laying on its back in mock funeral. Its face was pale, tallow like rendered fat. It was clearly dead. Not dead in the sense that a lifeless plastic doll should be, but like something that had once lived and was now denied the spark.

A box shifted just at the edge of the flashlight beam. Brad swung the light around. He could hear the tiny footfalls of the living doll running for cover in the surrounding darkness. The light fell on Todd's face. He was grinning still. His eyes were completely devoid of whites or irises; they were completely black. They were the same as Sarah's eyes on the night of the flood.

"Tell my father, he has something of mine," was all Todd said.

Brad stopped breathing. He watched as Todd took hold of the zipper on his sweatshirt. Slowly he unzipped it revealing the black t-shirt beneath. Brad dropped the beam of the light onto Todd's chest. In the center of the dark fabric of his shirt was a hole the size of a fist. The pale flesh around it was ripped and torn, broken splintered ribs jutted from the edges, stained with smeared blood. And deep inside yawned the empty cavity where Todd's heart used to reside. Todd held his sweatshirt open and stared back with that horrible smile. Blood seeped anew from the gaping hole in his chest.

Monster

    Brad gasped again, his mind reeling. He rolled over and sprang toward the door of the playroom.
    He left the flashlight rolling back and forth on the floor.

Christopher Cunningham

Chapter Nine

Brad ran as he'd never run before. No true thoughts occupied his mind, only images of the horrors he'd seen. The monstrous Leviathan, the mutilated boy, even the creepy doll scurrying in the dark, sent electric waves of nausea through his gut. He sprinted in darkness, back in the direction from which he'd come earlier. Straight down the hallway, past the basement alcove and the therapy pool, straight into the lobby. He didn't see Sister Kayla at her reception desk. It didn't register whether she was there or not. All he saw were the front doors. All he wanted was escape. All he hoped for was this insanity to end. He hit the front doors, barely slowing down. They flew open before him, and he was immediately hit by an incredibly bright light.

As if that light were a physical barrier, Brad jerked to a halt. He threw his arms and hands up to shield his embattled eyes. As they began to adjust, he realized that it was daylight that blinded him. Once again, his thoughts spun disoriented. A second earlier, as he raced toward the glass doors, he could see only the darkness of night, now it was full daylight - no sunrise, no dawn. He looked up and saw the sun high above in the stark blue sky. Brad blinked and slowly lowered his shielding arms.

The gravel parking area spread out before him. It was surrounded by bright green manicured lawn. Brad could smell the grass as if it were freshly cut. He could see where the gardens began and where the gravel road ran off and disappeared into the forest. The trees there were thick with foliage, darker green than the grass, but the wood beneath was darker still. Spindly trunks stood in staccato lines along the edge, banishing the entry of the new light of day. Its long barrier loomed ominous and unwelcoming.

One of the doors behind him opened and someone stepped out. Brad spun around feeling someone touch his shoulder. It was Antony. His dark angular features appeared concerned.

"Hey, I've been looking all over for you," Antony said. "I saw you running. Is everything okay?"

Brad exploded. He pictured Antony holding the blade he'd used to kill his son. He had the terrible vision of Todd and his ruined and gaping chest. Brad swung his fist and struck Antony defenseless in his face. The blow knocked Antony off balance, and he tumbled down the stone steps. Brad rushed to follow him. Antony landed on his back in the gravel and Brad knelt over him and punched him again. Blood spewed from Antony's shattered nose. Antony looked up at him dazed. Brad punched him again.

Suddenly, he was grabbed from behind.

Hands slipped beneath his armpits, and he was lifted with no effort. He hung, feet dangling above the gravel, then was set back to the ground. He was surrounded by black and white garments. Sister Kayla and another nun rushed to kneel around Antony. Father Gabraulti was beside him. And behind Brad was Sister Monica. It seemed that the old woman had been the one to stop his assault and lift him from the ground.

"Mr. Turner, that's enough!" said Gabraulti. It was the first time he'd said anything outside his normal range of calm.

"This bastard killed his son!" Brad tried to shake off Sister Monica's grasp, but she was far too strong.

On the ground below, Antony began to cry.

"He's right. I'm so sorry. I had to do it. I had no choice," he pleaded to the circle of faces around him. Then he turned to Brad, and a look of realization came across him. His voice raised with excitement. "You were there, weren't you? You saw it. You know what it is. You know I had no choice. You would have done the same. You would have...You would have done the same!"

The Sisters laid their hands on Antony's shoulders trying to comfort him. Kayla held a white handkerchief at his bloody nose.

Gabraulti lifted his eyes from Antony and turned to Brad. "We know, Mr. Turner. We all know what Antony has done. That's why he's here. Redemption is a long road and we're here to help with the journey. It's not for us to judge."

Brad relaxed. He stopped fighting Sister Monica's restraint. He was exhausted. He remembered the awful Leviathan and he wondered if he could have denied its terrible will. He wondered if he would have done what Antony had done. Was Antony right about him? He didn't want to admit even to himself that it was possible.

Gabraulti nodded to Monica, and she released her grip.

"Why don't we get you both back to your rooms," the priest suggested. "You're tired, the rest will do you good." He turned to his female companions. "Sisters, will you assist Mr. Sharpe?"

"Yes, Father," they responded.

Gabraulti escorted Brad back to his room. Neither of them spoke as they made their way there. Brad sat on the edge of his bed; he could feel the metal frame through the thin mattress. His head ached. He had so many questions, but he knew that asking them might only reveal his own spiral into insanity.

Brad's grandmother had struggled with mental illness. He remembered visiting her at various facilities in his youth - quiet, sterile hospital rooms much like this one. He recalled his grandmother's stories about the little guardian angels that looked after everyone from afar. But as he grew older, these stories took a strange turn. They slowly filled with visions of demons and bizarre demands. Demands that she began to follow, to the dismay of his parents. In time, her behavior escalated to the point where increased medications and occasional hospital stays were all they could do to keep her safe. But eventually the madness won out. Brad's grandmother died a raving lunatic strapped to a hospital bed, much like the one upon which he sat. Brad worried now that she had passed more to him than memories, myths, and superstitions. Perhaps he was on the same track that led his grandmother to ruin.

"I'm so sorry, Father," he said.

Gabraulti stood across from him. He was tall and seemingly untouched by the strangeness that infected this place. He smiled. "It's alright," he began. "Antony will survive. In some ways, he wants to be punished for what he's done. He'll forgive you. He may actually thank you."

"Yeah, I suppose," Brad answered. "But that's not what I mean. I'm sorry about everything, especially about what happened to Ray. I'm not sure I remember it right, but I know I didn't want to hurt him. I didn't want things to end up the way they did."

"Ray?" said Gabraulti. "Is that your son's name?"

"Ray, the big guy from therapy… the swimming pool?"

Gabraulti stood silent with a compassionate, but very confused and questioning smile.

Brad gave up. "Thank you, Father, I think I'd like to lay down now, get some rest."

"Of course. I'll come and check on you later." He turned and left the room pulling the door partly closed behind him.

Brad laid back on the bed. He pulled his feet up without removing his shoes. As exhausted as he felt, he doubted that sleep was an option. He stared at the ceiling. It was in disrepair. Like the walls, it had missing plaster where he could see into the dark spaces between the joists. In the corner closest to him, the plaster bulged in a hanging dome. It sagged as if filled with thousands of tiny spiders. It seemed poised like a pulsing boil ready to pop. The unpleasant thought made his stomach turn and he tried to push it away. He closed his eyes.

Immediately he felt the familiar pressure in his chest. He wasn't sure whether it came and went, or if he had simply learned to ignore it when distracted by other thoughts. He tried to remember when he first began to feel the weight of it. Maybe it was the night that he had almost been caught with Valarie in his apartment. At one time he thought that was the scariest moment of his life. A sardonic chuckle came to him as he pondered how wrong he'd been about that. He decided that the first time he'd really noticed the pressure was later than that, when things really started to go bad.

Brad remembered arriving at the *Buy-4-Less* for his shift the day after Sarah and Jason came back from their trip. It was a morning like any other. He walked through the aisles to the office in the back. Bennie, the 1st assistant manager was there. His large bulk swiveled around in his chair as Brad grabbed his timecard and punched in. It was 9:06 AM and Bennie already held a half-eaten microwave burger in his greasy squat fingers. He had a funny look on his face as he watched Brad replace his card.

"What's up, Bennie?" Brad said to him.

"Hey Brad," Bennie continued his stare.

"What's going on? Is there a problem?"

"You tell me." Bennie shoved another bite of food into his mouth.

Brad huffed at him. "Cut the shit, Bennie. What's up?"

"I don't know what went on between you and Valerie last night, but she's talking some smack about it this morning. Look, it's none of my business what you do on your own time. But when Paul finds out you're fooling around with another employee, he's going to be pissed."

That was it. That's when Brad first noticed the pressure. Maybe it was there before. Maybe it had already started growing, like roots slowly attacking a concrete foundation, tearing it apart chip by chip, grinding structure to sand. But there was no mistaking it now. His lungs felt turned to stone. For some stupid reason he thought he had dodged this bullet the night before. Obviously, he was wrong.

"Wait a minute," Brad defended. "I'm not fooling around with anybody. Whatever Valarie's saying, she's got it wrong."

Bennie held up his shiny hands. "Like I said, it's none of my business. But you better go talk to her and get your stories straight. Paul's coming in at 10:00, and you know store policy."

"Yeah, I know, I know God damn it," Brad shook his head. "Thanks for the heads-up, Bennie. I'll go talk to her now."

Brad knew exactly where Valerie would be. He found her at one of the two check-out registers. This early in the morning there were few customers in the store. Valerie was talking quietly to Tracie who stood at the next counter. Tracie glared at Brad as he approached.

"Can I talk to you for a minute?" he asked Val.

She spun around tugging her *Buy-4-Less* apron down tight, then punched her hands to her hips. "What?... about what you did to me last night?"

"Can we talk in private?" he lowered his voice.

"If you want to talk, we can do it right here," she insisted.

"Good morning, Mrs. Barnes. How are you this morning?" Brad heard Tracie say as an elderly customer began to place items on the adjacent conveyor.

"Can you step over here, please?" he asked Val a little more forcefully.

Valerie huffed now. She stomped over to where the ice machine sat by the front windows. "What?" she said.

Brad began in little more than a whisper. "Listen, about last night. I'm sorry I had to send you out the window. That was not cool. But there was no way I could have explained to my wife why you were there, in our bedroom. I panicked, okay? Besides, nothing happened, right? I mean, between us. Nothing happened."

"What do you mean, nothing happened? You tried to take advantage of me, that's what happened."

His breath caught in his throat. "What do you mean by that? I didn't take advantage of you. Hell, you're the one that showed up at my house, remember? What are you talking about?"

Val looked at him stern faced. "I want a raise," she said. "At least $5.00 more an hour. And I don't want to work weekends anymore."

"Wait a minute," Brad said. "I can't do that. I'm just the 2nd assistant manager. There's no way. I don't have the authority." He started to realize what was happening. His chest tightened.

"$6.00 an hour," she raised. "Otherwise, I tell Paul you've been touching me in the storeroom. He'll believe that, you pervert."

"What the fuck are you talking about?" He tried to restrain the volume of his voice, but now the weight of extortion was bearing down.

"He won't believe that. I'm a married man, for Christ's sake!"

"I'll tell your wife too," she continued. "I'll tell her you've been fucking me and that I think I'm pregnant. She'll love that, won't she?"

"You fucking bitch!" he said too loudly.

He heard a gasp. Brad saw old Mrs. Barnes looking at him with a horrified expression. Tracie stood next to her glaring. Brad returned Mrs. Barnes stare with a guilty, apologetic smile, then he grabbed Valerie's arm and walked her a few feet further away.

"Listen, you can't do this. I can't get you a raise. I mean, I can recommend something, but a $6.00 increase? That's crazy. Nobody's getting that much. Not even me and Bennie. Come on, be reasonable."

She frowned and raised a single eyebrow. "$2.00," she said. "But I still don't want to work weekends."

Brad closed his eyes, took a deep breath. The pressure against his chest was enormous. "I'll see what I can do, but I can't make you any promises."

"You have until the next schedule comes out," she said. "Nobody treats me the way you did. Take care of it or I swear I'll tell everybody what you did." She turned and went back to her station leaving Brad standing there with his mouth hanging half open.

Now, he was sure. That was when he'd first noticed the pressure, like his ribs were squeezing the lifeblood from his vital organs. He remembered wondering if he were having a heart attack. Maybe an embolism was about to break loose and wander through his body like a torpedo in search of a target. He remembered watching Val walk away from him and feeling anger turn to true hatred. This spoiled, obnoxious, narcissistic bitch was going to ruin his life. She would get him fired from his job and drive Sarah and his child away. There would be nothing left for him. He'd have to start his life all over. Looking back that may have been a blessing, but at that moment its weight was crushing. If only he had not answered the door when she called on him that night. If only he'd made another choice.

As he lay on the antique hospital bed, eyes closed and reliving these memories, music drew him back to the moment. It was a beautiful sound, like a choir of whistlers each playing their own part in perfect harmony. He relaxed. His blood pressure fell and the weight on his chest dispersed. The melody he heard was familiar. He was sure it was something he had heard a thousand times before. He could anticipate each note, each run of notes falling like cascading waters. But no matter how hard he tried; he could not identify the tune.

"Mal! Is that you, Mal?" he spoke loudly through the opening in the doorway.

The door pushed open and Mal Livengood stood in the threshold. He wore his green work clothes and black belt. His face was lit by his contagious smile. He lifted his black brows high over his dark eyes. The head of his mop lay deep in his rolling bucket, and he leaned on the tall handle.

"Mr. Turner, how are you today?" he said ending his tune.

Brad sat up and smiled.

"A moment ago, I would have told you I felt like I've been lost in some kind of Hell, but to tell you the truth, right now I'm feeling better." Brad waved him in. "Do you have a minute? I could sure use some company."

"For you?" Mal still smiled. "Of course, I do." He leaned his mop handle against the wall and stepped into the room. He sat sideways at the foot of the bed.

"It's been difficult, hasn't it?" Mal asked.

Brad nodded to him. "Oh my God, yeah," he answered. "I feel like I'm losing my mind. It's crazy, I know, but I feel like you're the only one I can talk to. Like you're the only anchor I have to reality."

Mal laughed softly. "Well, I don't know about that," he shrugged as if flattered. "I just meant that it's tough to be stuck in a strange place. And there's a lot of strange folk about. I can see how it could make someone feel... out-of-sorts."

"Out-of-sorts?" Brad chuckled. "I can't tell you how true that is. I've seen some crazy stuff. I'm afraid to even talk about it." Brad paused for a moment, weighing a decision.

"Listen, I want to ask you something. Just to see if I really am losing my mind," Brad continued timidly.

"Go ahead," said Mal.

"The pool? Did you see me at the pool last night?"

"The pool?" Mal asked.

Brad's spirits dropped.

Mal looked back over his shoulder at the open doorway. No one seemed to be around. "I took care of that for you," he said quietly. "I cleaned everything up. You don't need to worry about that."

Brad lit up again. "We're talking about Ray, right? Ray, in the pool?" Brad whispered.

"Yes," Mal said. "You don't need to worry about it."

"Oh my God," Brad relaxed his posture. "I said something to Gabraulti earlier and he acted like he'd never heard of the guy. I thought I... I totally lost it."

Mal nodded his head affirmatively, but he held a finger to his lips.

"Sorry," Brad said in a whisper. "You just don't know how good that makes me feel - Not what happened at the pool. That was horrible. But that even if I might be losing it, at least I'm not totally crazy." His mind was racing. "Mal, you've got to tell me. What is this place? What the hell is going on here? You said something before, like, it's not what it appears to be, or something like that. What did you mean? What is this place?"

Mal gritted his teeth and furrowed his brow. "Mr. Turner, I'd like to help you, but… I just work here. It's not really my place to interfere. In fact, it's against the rules."

"Okay," Brad said taking the cue. "That's something. What are the rules? Who makes them? Come on Mal, please. I have to know."

Mal looked down between his knees and slowly shook his head.

"Okay," Brad continued a little calmer now. "Then just tell me this. What is that thing? I know you know what I mean. At least, I think you do. That monster out there? Maybe it's all in my head. I've tried to convince myself that it is. But I feel like it has something to do with all of this. Everything that's happening. I can't figure out what it wants. It's got me so scared, so overwhelmed. It makes everything seem so… I don't know. It's like there's no words to describe it. It makes my head want to explode. Is it really just in my head? Am I just imaging it?"

Mal cringed at the question. He stood up and walked to the door. He took hold of his mop handle and stopped there with his back to the room. He looked back over his shoulder. "I'm sorry," he said, then he began to push the rolling bucket back out into the hall. "I wish I could…I can't help you. It's not my place."

Brad jumped up and raced to the doorway. "Mal wait!" he said quietly. "I'm sorry, but… what about my family? Can you tell me anything about them?"

Mal turned and faced him. He no longer glowed. He looked pensive, his expression sad, but compassionate. "The answers you're looking for are here," he said. "You'll find them in time, whether you want to or not. That's why you're here. There are choices that have to be made, and no one can help you. Certainly not me. It's up to you, Mr. Turner. It's all up to you."

"Mal, what the fuck does that mean?" Brad touched his arm.

"It's getting late," Mal said. "And I've got a lot to do. These floors don't clean themselves, you know." He turned away and started rolling the mop bucket down the hall in front of him. Once again, he began to whistle, but it was a different tune now, still familiar, but its mood was now droning and downcast.

Brad stepped back into his room, trying to process the conversation. He was more confused now than before. Then something Mal said before leaving caught his attention. *"It's getting late,"* was what he said. Brad wondered what he meant. Late for what? He'd only been back in his room for an hour, maybe less.

He turned and faced the window. It was dark again. Somehow the day had passed him by, and another long night was before him.

Slowly, the creeping pressure returned to his chest.

Chapter Ten

Brad backed away from the window in his room. The thin stained curtains hung open. They shifted almost imperceptibly as if made from a fabric of ghostly mist. The glass sash between was closed, so that no outside air drove their faint movement. Framed there he could see his own reflection in the smooth black glass. He saw himself as he had thousands of times before. Other than the dark shadow of whiskers on his face and the chaos of unkempt hair on his head, he looked as he always had. In fact, he was surprised by how normal he did appear. Part of him expected to see a madman standing in the reflection. A man on the verge, out of his mind, ready to erupt raving and out of control. In many ways, that is how he felt inside. That was what surprised him. From the outside he couldn't see what was happening within. The madness was hiding under his skin, like the remnant of a nightmare unshared.

Suddenly empowered by this costume of calm, he drew in a deep breath. He could imagine the oxygen feeding his bloodstream and coursing through him. He raised himself up to his full height. He needed to stay strong if he were going to survive this place. If Mal was right, then he wouldn't have to keep searching for the answers he so desperately wanted. Somehow, they would find him. But he couldn't just sit and wait. He was driven to go on. He needed to find his family.

Brad turned from the window and saw a door framed between his bed and the bathroom. Through his entire occupancy there had been no door there. He approached it cautiously noticing its scratched paint and chipped wood. It matched its surroundings. He blinked his eyes testing their veracity.

Carefully, he peered around the edge of the wall where the door was mounted. The bathroom was on the other side. It was unchanged. The pink tiled walls, the sink and medicine cabinet, the shower stall and toilet, they were all there. But where the phantom door should have connected, there was only tile.

Back in the room, Brad stood in front of the door. Warily he reached out and touched it. It felt real beneath his fingers, cold as ice. Curiously he knocked on it with his knuckles. He waited tensely but no one answered. After a moment, he crept closer and pressed his ear against the cold surface. At first, he heard only the seashell echo of silence. But then, something more. It was a voice. Far off, like a distant whisper in an empty church. But it was familiar. Like the voice he'd heard echoed through the telephone lines, it was indecipherable and obscured. But he knew that voice, it was Sarah. Brad's heart filled with adrenaline. He grabbed the door handle without thinking more and pulled it open.

In a moment of pure vertigo, he found himself standing at the top of a steep narrow stairway delving deep into darkness below. It was an arched passage, stone like the tunnel he had explored before. Cast iron brackets again held candles that flickered dim light into the depths. Now there was no mistaking that he could hear the distant voice of the mother of his child.

"Sarah," he called out in the loudest of whispers. His voice drained down the stone stair. He tried louder. "Sarah, it's me! It's Brad! Can you hear me?"

He turned his ear to the darkness and listened. He could hear her voice still, but it did not respond to him. It continued as if in conversation. As strange as this bizarre and unnatural portal was, even as it had appeared where it had no right to exist, he felt he had no choice but to enter, if only for the hope of finding his Sarah.

He began to descend the stairs. The sound of his feet tapped quickly against the stones. He used his hands against the cold walls to maintain his balance. The candles were spaced every ten feet or so, alternating on each side, and he started counting them as he went. When he reached twenty, he realized that he must be far underground now, deeper perhaps, than Mal's basement abode. He became convinced that he was in another altered reality, and he wondered what horrors awaited in the deep. Soon he came to a landing in a small rectangular room. At the far end was an arched doorway barred by a cast iron gate and flanked by two last candles.

Brad took a moment to look at the stone walls around him. He could sense fresh air flowing. Cautiously, he stepped up to the gate and grasped the iron bars. There appeared to be no latching mechanism. He looked behind him and saw that the stairwell had vanished. Nothing but an empty stone chamber remained. Unphased by the oddity, he swung open the gate and crossed the threshold.

He knew immediately where he was. He was back in the garden, though not in the same area as before. A tall circle of hedges, too high to see over, surrounded him. A flagstone path led forward from the archway and through an opening in the hedgerow. Brad stepped down from the threshold and looked around. The stone building sat alone in the center of the circle, its dimensions were the same small rectangular shape, a single story with slate roof. It reminded Brad of a small mausoleum in a churchyard cemetery. There was no mystical stairway leading from the back and extending toward the night sky.

But there were stars shining above. They were brighter and denser than any he had ever seen. Familiar constellations were absent, but in their place were patches of color, vast regions of gaseous nebula in purples, greens, and reds. It was like no sky he had ever seen. He stood for a moment captured by its beauty. Caught so off guard he almost forgot what led him here.

Then he heard her voice again. It came from out in the garden, beyond the high hedge. Brad wanted to call out to her, but he remembered the Gardeners. The giant hideous insects that tended these gardens, the awful cave crickets of his nightmares with their sharp clicking exoskeletons. He knew the danger of startling them, of setting off a panicked stampede of flying razor-sharp edges. If Sarah were out here, he didn't want to risk putting her in more danger. But if he could hear her voice, then surely, they could as well. He needed to find her before she set off their alarm.

Brad headed down the path. It took only a moment to realize that this was a hedge maze, purposely designed to confuse and delay. He rushed as quickly as he could, stopping every now and then to listen for Sarah's voice. A few times he heard her more clearly. He risked raising his whispered voice to call out to her, only to hear her again even further off. She was with someone, the flow of her voice confirmed that. And fortunately, nothing about her tone sounded as if she felt threatened or endangered.

Brad worried for her, nonetheless. He was coming to terms with this place. It was a sick reflection of frustration and teasing insanity. A dangerous place where the walls of reality were broken down and trust was a thing that could not be trusted. If she was here and he could not find her, then he would have failed her again. And that was something he could not accept.

As he turned the corner of another hedgerow, he heard her voice more clearly than ever. He knew she was just through the hedge beside him. He stopped.

"Sarah!" he whispered loudly. "Sarah, it's me, Bradley! Can you hear me?"

There was no change in her pattern of speech.

He tried again, louder this time. "Sarah! I'm here! I'm right here! Answer me! Are you alright?"

Again, he heard no change, no response.

He looked around. He knew that if he stepped away, if he tried to turn the next corner hoping to reveal her, that she would slip even further from him. This was a physical maze, but it was conniving, it wanted to confuse and torment. Somehow it could change. It could re-imagine itself and take any form it chose. This living garden would not allow him his desire, so Brad decided in defiance and desperation, that he would cheat its intent.

Brad faced the hedge and the direction of Sarah's voice. He drove his hands into the hedge and pried the branches apart. He heard them snap and flutter as he forced an opening and stepped into the dark gap. The branches scraped and scratched his arms and face, but he forced himself forward like a man plunging through a dense jungle. Elsewhere he'd seen the hedge was only two or three feet thick, but he'd passed farther than that already. He kicked with his knees and swam with his arms. He was making progress. He was moving, but still the hedge went on. The further he went, the thicker it became, until he needed all his strength to struggle forward.

Finally, he could see light ahead. The starry night cast a glow on an opening in the garden. As he pushed toward it, he felt the branches of the hedge reach out for him. They swirled like snakes around his arms, around his legs, around his throat. The more he struggled, the tighter they became. He was caught, trapped in their grip. He plunged one last time with the remainder of his strength, but he was hopelessly tangled in their iron grasp.

Unable to move further, his face was now only an inch from breaking through. He could see the open area beyond, the round hedgerow, the stone benches, and the two people sitting in conversation. Behind them sprang an enormous tree. It had a thick trunk of intertwined roots that grew like muscle fibers, its low branches spread overhead. Fruit hanging from the branches glowed like lanterns in the night.

Tears came to his eyes when he saw her. It was Sarah. She sat on a bench angled so that Brad could see her in profile. She looked unchanged from when last he saw her. He could hardly believe that she was here and alive. He understood at some level that this might all be a fantasy. He had been deceived many times since arriving here. But there was something about this encounter that convinced him. She was here, almost close enough to touch. He tried with every fiber of his body to break through this barrier and hold her. Somehow that embrace would change everything. His deep sense of loneliness and guilt would pass. Somehow, her touch would set him free.

He called out to her, but no sound came from his throat. As he tried to force air through his larynx the hedge branches around his throat grew tighter. He felt the choking tension squeeze. Like piano wire, it would twist and split his skin releasing his head from his shoulders. He had almost cheated the garden, but now at the final moment, it had denied him.

Brad understood that this was as far as he might go for now, so he relaxed and the tension around his throat relented as well. He could now only listen to the sound of her voice and try to understand what had happened to her, discover the fate of his son, and maybe find a way for them to escape this bizarre reality where they all seemed to be trapped.

"I still don't understand why I've had to wait so long," he heard her say. Her voice was polite and soft, unmistakably hers. "It seems like it's been such a long time already. Why couldn't I have just left right away? Was there a problem I don't know about? Can you tell me?"

She was talking to a man who sat beside her. His back was to Brad so that his face could not be seen. But after Sarah's request he turned revealing his own profile. It was Mal Livengood. His green uniform matched the dull color of the night garden. His black hair shined in the starlight. One could almost see the pinpricks of light reflected there. How he had come from Brad's room to be here in the Garden so quickly was a mystery that Brad chose to ignore for the moment. Finally, finding Sarah was the only thing that mattered.

"I'm sorry Ms. Sarah," Mal answered in his friendly lyrical voice. "But it's not my place to delve into other people's lives. People make their own choices. They have their own destinies. I have a simple job here, and I think I do it well. I keep the floors clean and polished. Shiny enough to see yourself. It's important, I think. People should be able to see themselves as they are. I would guess that you've had a chance to see yourself in a new way since you arrived here, haven't you? It's just my small part in the scheme of things, I suppose."

Sarah smiled at him like an old friend.

"Hmmm," she sighed. "I'm just glad the time is here. Will you be at the ceremony too?"

"No, I'm afraid I have other duties," he answered. "We have a few more minutes to wait though. I'll stay and walk with you when they're ready."

Sarah turned her gaze upward. "This is the most beautiful place. If I have to wait, then I'm glad to be here."

Brad listened to their words, but they did nothing to quell his confusion. In fact, they fed it.

At first, just seeing her, alive and well, brought joyful tears. Seeing that she was safe and unhurt was all he had hoped. Not only that, but she seemed content to be in this place. There was no sign of the distress that he had been going through. She was ready to go home. He knew that feeling well. But what was this ceremony? Was it some kind of celebration or ritual? What kind of ceremony was required to leave here?

Monster

No one had said anything to him about a ceremony. Sarah seemed to know more about this place than he did.

But it was not what she said that stuck in his mind, it was what she hadn't said. She didn't mention Brad at all. Maybe he was reading too much into the omission, but didn't she seem *too* content? After what had happened to them, the flood, the near drowning, the separation and isolation, everything they had been through, she seemed hardly concerned. This didn't seem like the woman he knew.

And what about their son? Where was Jason? He was never out of his mother's care. She adored that child more than any other precious thing on Earth. And here she was, sitting with a stranger in a strange garden, no husband, no child, no family at all to clutter her awed vison of an alien sky. How was this possible? Sarah was the most loving, caring, and positive person he had ever known. She had never once done a selfish thing in her life.

He was forced to admit that his last thought wasn't true.

But in any case, this was not the person he knew. Though, she was not an imposter. Somehow, he was sure of that. But something had changed. Something had turned her attention from the real things she once valued. Something misled her, deceived her. Something that would eventually lead her away from this place without her family. And being left behind, perhaps he and Jason would be lost forever.

And that thought led him to Mal, what was he doing? Didn't he have something to say about Brad? Or was he keeping it secret, like he seemed to have done with Brad about her? At least Mal was consistent. His answers to Sarah seemed just as cryptic as they'd been to him. But how could he not do something to ease Brad's suffering? To let him know that his wife was alive. Was it possible that Mal was doing him some service with his silence? Maybe Brad had it wrong. Maybe Sarah already knew he was alive, and she simply didn't care.

Brad needed more than ever to reach her. He had to have answers. He renewed his struggle against the living chains of the hedgerow. But he could make no more headway. If only he could break through. If he could take Sarah in his arms, hold her tight, and remind her of their love and the child they'd created. Then they might all be free. Free from this place and the nightmare it oozed and bled. Free to return to the simple life that he had learned to tolerate.

Suddenly and without warning, he felt something clutch at his clothes from behind. He was being pulled backward and away from his goal. His initial thought was of a Gardener with its hideous insect eyes, spotting his disfigurement of their beautiful hedge work. It would tear him apart like it would an invasive pest, dismembering him with its hatchet-sharp limbs, oblivious to all the plans and schemes of his sentient mind, and of the love and horrors of his beating heart.

Brad was tossed onto the maze pathway landing on his back with a thud. He raised his arms in blind defense, but nothing horrible happened.

"What are you doing? Are you crazy?" came the unexpected voice.

He looked through his upheld hands and saw Mary standing over him. She hovered there with a sea of stars and colored light framing her hair.

"What are you doing here?" he asked, now relieved that he was not about to become chopped fertilizer for the garden.

"I'm smoking a cigarette, you dolt." She raised her hand showing him the half-smoked butt with its rapidly spiraling string of smoke. "The garden's the only place where I can. I thought you knew that."

"Yeah...yeah I did." He extended his hand.

Mary leaned forward and helped pull him to his feet. He could see entirely down her blouse as she bent. Her firm breasts hung and swayed with her motion, natural and perfect in shape. Like a hypnotist might swing a shiny object before their subject's eyes, Brad was momentarily entranced. Now on his feet, he caught her eyes. She had a wicked smile on her face. She knew the focus of his attention. He released her hand and took a step back.

"Now, what the hell are *you* doing here?" she asked. "Did you get lost in the maze? You know, trying to cut through the hedge is cheating. Besides, I don't think it's possible. Look at your face. You're all scratched up."

"I was looking for my wife, Sarah," he answered. "She's here, right on the other side of this hedge. I saw her. But I couldn't get through. I tried, but I couldn't get through."

"No kidding?" said Mary with untethered sarcasm.

"Yeah, no kidding!" he snapped. "I knew it. I've been lied to this whole time. Sarah is here and I'm sure my son is too. I just need to get to her. We need to get out of here."

Mary crushed her cigarette butt with her bare foot on the flagstone path, then pulled another from a packet in the back pocket of her tight jeans. She struck a match and lit the cigarette. Matchstick sulfur filled the air. "I told you this place was fucked up. It'll fuck with your head something awful."

"I know," he said. "You gotta help me. You have to tell me what's going on. You know what's up. I know you do. Why do they want to keep us apart? What could they possibly hope to gain? Sarah was talking with Mal. She didn't seem to care. I don't know if she's even looking for me. She didn't even ask about our son. It doesn't make sense. Please, you've got to help me."

Mary still looked at him with a sideways smile. "My offer still stands," she said. "I'll tell you everything you want to know. You just need to take care of me first. We'll go back to my room, and you can be my little playdate. And when I'm done with you, I'll tell you whatever you want to know."

Brad squeezed his eyes shut and balled up his fists at his side. "No, you don't understand. I can't. What's the use of finding my family if I have to betray them to do it? I promised myself. I promised her that it would never happen again. I promised."

"*Really?*" Mary said raising her voice and her eyebrows together. "Never again, huh? You've been a bad boy before, hmmm? Oh, this is delicious," she smiled.

"Oh, Jesus Christ, Mary, why are you doing this? I mean, please. Can you just fucking help me? Please?" Brad dropped his shoulders.

Mary's self-satisfied smile faded. Her eyes softened. "Okay, I'll tell you what. I'll lead you out of the maze and get you back to the facility. I'll answer your questions. But I need something from you. I want to know what's got you so uptight. There has got to be a good story there. Nobody's ever turned these down." She swiveled gently with her shoulders so that her breasts swayed back and forth. Her wicked smile returned. "If your story is good enough, then maybe I'll tell you what you want to know. But it better be good, no bullshit, no holding back."

"Okay," Brad relented. "I'll tell you, but you better not be messing with me. Nobody knows what I'm about to tell you,

Monster

and no one can ever know. You'll understand why. It's between us, right?"

"Deal," she said. Her eyes lit up. She turned sideways and motioned for him to follow. "It's this way."

Brad nodded and walked beside her down the dark path. Then he began to tell his story.

Chapter Eleven

It was a Saturday, the same week that Valerie had confronted Brad. He had tortured himself for days over it. How could he have been so stupid? He felt caught in an inescapable maze. The only way to deal with this, he decided, was to tell Sarah the truth - the whole truth. He had run the incident with Valerie through his head a thousand times and kept coming to the same conclusion: he was guilty of stupidity, but not infidelity.

The flaw in this justification was that if Sarah had not come home when she did, the result may have been different. Who was he kidding? The result *would* have been different.

Of course, he realized that if he had slept with Valerie, his circumstance would be the same. She would still be trying to blackmail him. Given what he knew now, extortion was likely her plan from the start. It all made sense from that perspective. She had never shown any interest in him before. Then suddenly she showed up at his apartment, knowing that he was married and had a child, knowing that his family was out of town. He was also her boss, and that was bad no matter how you spun it. She'd recognized him as the dupe he was. It was a cluster-fuck, and he was caught in the middle. The irony was that Valerie had greatly over-estimated any benefit he could give her by extorting him. He had close to nothing, yet she had chosen to take even that away from him. He felt like a magnet for bad luck.

Regardless of the efficacy of her plan, Brad decided that he couldn't take the chance that she was bluffing. The damage she could do was real. The time to fess-up with Sarah was now, before the hammer came down.

"We need to talk," he said to Sarah that morning as she poured her first cup of coffee.

"Ewww, you sound so serious," she smiled.

He sat at their small kitchen table. His heart pounding in his chest so hard that he thought she might see it through his shirt. He had been awake for hours, daring himself to make this the moment. Now that he had opened his mouth, he wished that Jason would wake up and start to fuss. Then he could use that as an excuse to escape his decision.

"It is serious," he said.

Sarah's smiled faded. She was in her robe and pajamas, her hair flat from sleep. The cross around her neck caught a ray of light from the kitchen window. It was her big cross, her favorite, thin silver bars, three inches high and one across. It sent a beam streaking along the wall as she sat down across from him. She clutched it as she often did when she was worried. She stared patiently. A long silence followed.

"Something happened when you were away," he began. "I think I may be in trouble."

"Oh my!" she said. "What is it? What happened?" She reached across the table and gripped one of his hands.

"One of the girls down at my work. She's trying to blackmail me. She's threatening to tell lies about me. I don't know what to do."

Sarah squeezed his hand. "What do you mean, blackmail? What lies? What does she want from you?"

"She wants money. She wants me to give her a huge raise and fix her hours at work. I told her I couldn't do that. Then she threatened to tell the boss that I've been touching her... back in the storeroom. I swear it's not true, but that won't matter. If she tells Paul that, he'll have to fire me. How can he not?"

"Oh my God. Who is it? Who's saying these things?"

"It's Valerie. She's one of the cashiers down at the *Buy-4-Less*."

Sarah's face turned red. "She's one of those little sluts that you work with. I knew they were trouble!"

"But that's not all," he said. The wheels in Brad's head were turning. So far, Sarah didn't seem angry with him. She seemed to believe what he was saying. Of course she did, it was all true. Why wouldn't she believe him? But the next part of the story was the crux of it all. It was what he felt worst about. It was the make-or-break moment that he dreaded.

"She also said she was going to tell you," he began. "She said she was going to tell you that she was here when you were away, and that I had sex with her."

Sarah's eyes bulged.

"I swear to you that I didn't," he pled quickly. "I swear I didn't have sex with her. She's lying. I've been so afraid that you'd believe her. Afraid that you'd think I did, and that you'd leave and take Jason with you. She knew you were going to be gone. Bennie down at work told her. I'm sure he didn't know what she was up to. But she planned this, the fucking bitch. You should have seen the smug look on her face. She doesn't care at all. She'd be happy if she ruined our lives. Even if I could get her a raise, she'd keep holding this shit over me. Not that we have anything to give. She would still want more. What are we supposed to do? All she has to do is say it, and people will believe her. I'm screwed. I'm going to lose everything."

Sarah said nothing. Her face grew stern, and she stood up from the table, turning her back.

Brad watched her. His heart pounding. He could feel the awful pressure. This was the moment he feared. "Sarah?"

Sarah slowly turned around and faced him. "That fucking bitch," she said with a coldness that Brad didn't recognize. He'd never even heard her curse before, not like this.

"Has she said anything to your boss yet?" she asked.

"I don't think so," he answered. "She said that I have until the new schedule comes out. She doesn't want to work weekends anymore."

"Oh, that poor thing," Sarah's sarcasm was sharp as a claw. "When does the schedule come out?"

"Today," he answered. "It's Saturday. She'll see it today when she comes in. I don't know what she'll do. Maybe she'll try to push me again. Maybe she'll give up. I don't know. I've got to be there in half an hour. I suppose I'll find out."

"Yeah, you do that," Sarah seemed absent. She started talking as if to herself.

"She won't tell your boss yet. It won't do her any good to have you fired. You can't get her what she wants if you're fired. She'll try me first. She'll try to drive us apart. She'll try and bleed us dry first, then she'll tell your boss. She may try to sue the business or threaten to. That's probably her best play, but she'll save that for last."

Brad had survived his admission and now he didn't know what to think. He'd never seen this side of Sarah before, so cold and calculating. He wondered if she might be in a mild state of shock. It was like someone else was under her skin. But her surprising reaction seemed secondary now that the worst was over. He had come clean - mostly. Sarah never needed to know that Valerie had been in their apartment. It was another one of her lies. There was no need for Sarah to suffer further from his bad decisions.

"Thank you for believing me," he said to her. He reached out and pulled her toward him. He hugged her around her waist from his seated position. "I love you and I never want to hurt you. I swear I'll never let anything like this happen again. Never. I'll never let anyone come between us or take advantage of us. I swear."

Sarah stroked his hair gently. "You better get ready for work," she said absently. "Jason will be up soon, and I've got some thinking to do."

Sarah's reaction was unexpected. He really had never seen her like this before. But his focus was elsewhere. He realized he might actually keep his family, though his job might be a different story. He didn't think that Valerie would just go away. But maybe if he and Sarah acted together, then Valerie would give up and leave them alone. He couldn't say. For now, he was simply glad that the first hurdle was behind him.

Monster

When he arrived at work, he found that only one register was open. He questioned Tracie and discovered that Valerie had not shown up as expected. Brad found himself covering the other register until almost noon. When he finally had a break, he went back to the office and found Bennie sitting at the manager's desk. There was a half-eaten cherry pie balanced next to a stack of timesheets and order forms. Some of them had sticky red fingerprints on their corners.

"Well, look who's here," Bennie said to Brad.

"I've been here for three hours," Brad replied. "You'd know that if you weren't hiding back here all day. I've been up front covering for Valerie at the register. I guess she's a no-show?"

"Oh no, she showed up alright. And she looked pissed," Bennie wore a big obnoxious grin. "I thought you two had worked out your little spat?"

"Jesus, Bennie. When was she here? What happened? What did she say?"

"I don't know, 'bout a half-hour ago. She didn't say anything. She came in, looked at the new schedule, then she huffed and went straight out the back door. I figured it had something to do with you, so I didn't say anything. You better watch yourself. That girl is trouble."

"Yeah, no shit Bennie. Listen, you need to cover for me. I need to go do something."

"Hold on just a minute now," Bennie said. "You're forgetting who's the 1st assistant manager here."

"Fuck you, Bennie. Just cover for me. I'll be back as soon as I can." With that, Brad went out the back door himself.

Behind the *Buy-4-Less* there was a service alley. Here was the employee entrance and the loading dock. A chain-link fence separated the concrete way from a few acres of woodland, scattered with litter and abandoned shopping carts. The hidden alley was a haven for rats and cockroaches. This time of year, the stink of rotten produce was usually mild, but the last week or so had been warmer than usual and the dumpsters were getting ripe. When the garbage trucks came, refuse spilled onto the concrete and left a compressed slime of blackened lettuce on the slippery surface. Brad stepped carefully, trying not to lose his grip or soil his shoes.

As he passed the dumpsters, he saw his car parked there in the alley. It made him stop in his tracks. He never drove to work. His commute was a five-minute walk. A figure moved beyond the windshield. As he squinted to see who was there, the door opened, and Sarah stepped out. He could hear Jason screaming from the back seat. The boy's cries became muted as she slammed the door closed and walked toward Brad.

"Sarah, what are you doing here?"

Her face was sullen and ashy in color. "I wanted to have a talk with that bitch," she said without elaboration.

"She's already gone," Brad told her. "Bennie said she left already. I didn't see her."

"I've been waiting here," she said. "I was afraid to come inside."

"Why, what's going on?"

Sarah turned her head and looked at the ground beyond where Brad was standing.

Brad looked behind him and saw something laying between two of the dumpsters. Valerie was splayed on her back among the filth. She wore the same winter coat she had at his apartment. Her knit cap lay on the ground not far away. She was unmoving. A puddle of blood flowed from her head toward a nearby drain. It was already growing sticky, oozing like cherry filling.

"I saw her when she came out," said Sarah. "I told her that we weren't intimidated by her. I told her we were going to make sure *she* got fired. She cursed and tried to hit me. So, I pushed her. She slipped and fell backward and hit her head on the dumpster."

Brad's heart raced. The pressure on his chest was nearly suffocating. On the sharp top corner of one of the dumpsters there was a stain of blood and a small clump of hair and scalp. He stood over Valerie; the color drained from his face.

"Is she dead?"

"I think so. She hasn't moved at all. That's why I'm waiting for you. You need to help me."

"Help you? What? What do you mean?"

"You need to help lift her up, put her in the back of the car. We need to get rid of her."

"Oh shit…" he said.

"Come on Bradley. We need to do this before somebody sees her. This is going to look bad, really bad."

"Oh my God… people know what she was up to. Bennie, Tracie, God knows who else. People are gonna think we killed her on purpose. Oh shit!"

"That's why we need to get rid of her. Now before anybody sees. We need to get rid of her body. Pick her up and I'll get the trunk."

Brad obeyed her without thinking. His movements felt remote controlled. His mind was clouded. Brad knelt and lifted the limp body. She was light as a feather. He scanned the alley and the woods as he went, trying not to slip and fall himself on the slimy concrete. As Sarah raised the hatchback, Jason's screams blasted out from the backseat of the car.

When Brad lowered Valerie's body into the compartment, he noticed that there was a shovel and a tarp already inside. His mind was too awash and numb to question it.

Sarah rushed around to the passenger door. "Come on, let's go!"

Brad slammed the hatch and got in the car.

They drove, hours into the country. Winding roads through the high Appalachian hills. Neither of them spoke. Brad ran through everything that happened, over and over, one nightmare bleeding into the next. This was all his fault. And now he had drawn Sarah into it. This positive, loving, God fearing woman. Even if they somehow got away with this, what he had done would damn her to a lifetime of guilt and regret.

But he worried more about being caught. They would be arrested and convicted. They would spend their lives in prison. Jason would be parentless, raised by grandparents who would always blame Brad for their fate. All their past hatred toward him would be justified. And they would plant those seeds of hate in Jason. His son would grow up believing his father was a criminal, an adulterer, and a murderer.

After a long search, Brad found what he was looking for. He turned off the lonely mountain road they'd been following and onto an overgrown dirt track that appeared to have been long abandoned. The woods were deep and untouched, not even a beer can or a plastic bag in sight. He pressed forward slowly, pushing over saplings and brush with the front of their vehicle until they could go no further. Brad turned off the ignition and got out of the car. Sarah stepped out on the other side. Neither of them reacted to the continued screaming of their child.

There was a small stream near Brad's side of the car. Dull sunlight trickled in its narrow run. The trees around them were barren like skeletal arms reaching for the gray sky. The forest was not overly dense, but large boulders and fallen trees and brush piles made the area feel private and secluded. A vulture circled high above and drew a shadow across the scene. Not far away, Sarah was already searching the ground with her feet, pushing away leaves, trying to find the perfect spot to dig. It didn't take long before she found it.

"Over here," she said. "The ground's not as hard over here. Bring her, and the shovel too!"

Brad moved like a sloth to the back of the vehicle and popped the hatch. Valerie lay unmoving there, curled as he'd left her in the fetal position. Her hair was matted with thick, dark, blackish blood which collected on the tarp beneath her. He lifted her body from the trunk. She was light enough that he tossed her over his shoulder so that his hands were free to carry the shovel and tarp as well. Brad closed the trunk only to deaden the sound of frustrated screaming from his son.

He dropped Valerie onto the leaf covered ground with a hollow thud. The sound made him nauseous. He stifled a gag, tasting the rising bile.

"Over here," Sarah pointed. "There aren't any roots in the way."

He let the tarp drop to the ground and then walked over to where Sarah stood. "I'll dig the hole. You go over and roll her up in the tarp."

Sarah looked like she was about to say something but remained silent. She walked away as he plunged the shovel into the thawed ground.

He dug with purpose. He wanted this to be over as quickly as possible. He just wanted to get back home. He knew that there would be some explaining to do, but so long as he and Sarah had their stories straight there wouldn't be a problem. They'd traveled so far that Valerie's body would never be found. There would be no proof that she was even dead. It would be just another missing person, another young person run off to start a new life somewhere. Who could prove otherwise?

Mentally, Brad was exhausted. He never could have imagined anything like this. It was nearly impossible to wrap his head around. But he was committed. If he were going to dig a grave, then it was going to be deep. No rummaging animal would disturb these bones. If Valerie was going to disappear, then he would make sure she stayed that way forever.

As he continued to dig, he heard the crumpling of the plastic sheet. Sarah unfolded the tarp and placed it on the ground beside the body. He heard shuffling, more wrinkling of plastic and an astonished cry. He looked over and saw Valerie reaching up, grasping Sarah by her hair with both hands. Valerie was still alive.

The women started screaming, wrestling with each other, Valerie on her back and Sarah on her knees above her. Valerie pulled Sarah down and rolled over onto her. She slapped with her hand and snagged Sarah's cross and its chain from around her neck, breaking the tiny links. It caught a flash of light as it flew to the ground beside them. Sarah gasped and clutched at her neckline.

Valerie used the distraction to roll off her. She tumbled briefly then got to her feet. But instead of running off into the woods, she ran directly toward Brad. He held the shovel with both hands in front of him like a bar to shield off an attack. But as she rushed toward him, he saw the terror in her eyes. They were wild and wide.

"Help me!" she cried.

Valerie ran into the shovel handle as if she hadn't noticed it. She reached out with her arms trying to find shelter in Bradley's arms.

Brad was frozen. His mind went blank. None of this seemed real.

"Please, don't let her kill me," she cried. "Please…"

Then Sarah appeared. She was directly behind Valerie. With one hand she grabbed Valerie's hair and yanked her head back. With the other hand she held her silver cross. Only an inch of its metal upright protruded from the bottom of Sarah's clenched fist, but it was enough. Sarah plunged it into the side of Valerie's neck, stabbing inward, then pulling back, ripping flesh as it went. She hammered with the thin metal bar puncturing her over and over again. Blood gushed and pumped from the tearing wounds in her neck and the artery beneath.

Brad stood immobile, inadvertently holding Valerie in place with the shovel handle. Just inches away from her face, her torment, her begging eyes. Then in an instant those eyes were vacant. Just like that, there was no longer anything behind them. The light within was gone. Sarah jerked her backward and Valerie dropped to the forest floor. She lay gurgling and twitching reflexively between them.

Sarah stood in a wide stance, her chest heaving and blood dripping from her attack hand. "Now you're dead, you fucking bitch!" Sarah cursed at her.

Brad stood paralyzed. This wasn't real. It couldn't be. But it was. Disposing of a body, the body of an enemy killed in a tragic accident was one thing. It was horrible and mind numbing. But murdering someone, an intentional killing, was entirely different. He was sick with nausea and acidic adrenaline. The poison of hatred pumped in his heart and spread throughout his body. But it was self-hatred. It was all about him. His actions set this in motion. It was about his inadequacies, his failings, his inhumanity. He was the contagion of bankrupt morality and he'd passed it to Sarah, infecting her with the wrath that he himself was too weak to become.

Sarah bent over and grabbed Valerie by her coat and started dragging her body back to where the tarp lay. "Keep digging!" she said.

Brad was still frozen in place.

Sarah let Valerie's corpse drop limp on the tarp. She looked at Brad and her grim expression faded. "It's okay, now we know she's dead. It's not like we could have let her go. Not after dragging her all the way out here in the trunk of our car. We didn't have a choice. She deserved this. She was trying to hurt us and our family. We had to stop her. She would have ruined everything."

Brad nodded robotically. He turned and continued to dig.

When he was done, they rolled Valerie's wrapped body into the grave and covered it with dirt. They camouflaged the site with leaves and sticks. The two of them knelt silently at the small stream and washed the dirt and blood from their hands.

Monster

Finally, they got back into the car, quietly and gently pulling the doors closed so as not to wake the baby. Jason had finally exhausted himself and fallen to sleep. It was early evening as Brad carefully reversed the car back out the dirt track to the road.

He felt a slight relief as they rolled onto the smooth pavement and began to accelerate. There was a tangible feeling that something had changed. There was a finality to this horrific episode being over, and now he could begin to try and cope with what they'd done. There was a part of him that hoped that they would never have to speak of it. If they could live in unspoken denial, then they might convince themselves that it never happened. That it was only a horrific dream.

A few hundred yards from where they pulled onto the road, around a slight bend, a rusty pick-up truck was parked off the shoulder. Tightness squeezed Brad's chest. His hands cramped, gripping the steering wheel. He slowed down as they passed.

It was an empty, dented, blue Ford with West Virginia plates. There were red stains near the tailgate and on the rear bumper. In the back window were decals of deer antlers and the NRA. There was an empty gun-rack mounted high behind the seat.

As they drove past, Jason woke up and started screaming again.

And above them, dark clouds began to gather before the smell of coming rain.

Chapter Twelve

Brad and Mary emerged from the hedge-maze. They were still deep in the garden, but now they could see its expanse and the dark looming presence of the Sanitarium. The black dome of night sky was scattered in patches of vibrant luminous color. Stars twinkled and pulsed, others shot in trails marking the curved abyss. Beneath it all, Brad and his companion stopped in a circular sitting area wrapped with benches and spoked hedge-lined paths. The night flowers rose in full bloom, but the sweet scent went unnoticed after the tale Brad had just told.

"That's the most fucked up story I've ever heard," said Mary. Her eyebrows arched high. She shook her head with a half-smile on her face. "And that girl of yours. She sounds like a psychopath if you ask me. You need to let that go."

"That's none of your business," he snapped at her. "Everything she did, she did for me, to protect us, and our family."

"If you say so," Mary admitted. "Like you said, it's none of my business."

Brad sat down heavily on one of the benches. This was the first time he allowed himself to really think about what happened. He'd pushed it down deep and buried it beneath everything that had happened since. It was still so recent. Had it been only three days? Four maybe? He couldn't tell how much time had passed in this strange place.

But Mary was right. What Sarah had done was crazy. In a million years he couldn't have imagined the fury he'd seen in her or the cold chill of her justification. It was his fault. He was the one who created the circumstances that set this in motion, not Sarah.

Even so, what he'd seen was beyond him. He could never have done what he'd seen her do. He didn't have it in him. At his most angry he had punched Antony. That was the first time in his life he had ever hit anyone, and it already bothered his conscience. But that was at the height of a stress that seemed unimaginable. He cursed this place and the way it played with his mind.

In retrospect, it seemed that Sarah had just snapped. He'd never seen any sign of the dark homicidal rage that he witnessed. He tried to ignore signs that it might have been premeditated – like the tarp, the shovel. His mind flashed to the memory of the flood, sitting beside her in their car. He remembered seeing those black eyes, her inhuman movements. Like something else was inside her, hidden beneath her actions. He forced the idea from his mind. It made his head ache. Focus - he had to focus. He needed to find her and save them both.

"It must be hard," Mary began. "To love someone so much, but to hate them at the same time."

Her words struck hard like a slap across the face of his psyche. He had no good response. There was no defense to that. His face burned as he looked down at his feet.

"Alright," he said exhausted. "Now it's your turn. You promised to tell me about this place. What it is and why I'm seeing what I'm seeing."

"Yeah, about that," she said with a blushing grin. "I'm not really sure what you think I can tell you. I mean, there's the obvious. Saint Lucius is an old hospital for people that are off their rockers. Used to be well-known, I guess. I think even the church has kind of forgotten about it, left it to die."

"That's not what I mean," he said. "You know what I'm talking about, all the weird shit that's going on."

"Well, like I said. People who come here are here for a reason. It's a hospital, a looney bin. Don't you think it's obvious why you're here? Especially after that wild story. You want to know why you're seeing weird shit? How could you not?"

"No!" he tried to restrain his tone. "That's not it! I didn't come here for treatment. I didn't come here by choice at all, and I wasn't brought here either. I just... wound up here somehow. I don't remember. We had an accident. We got caught in a flood... I'm just trying to find my family. I'm not crazy. I just want to find my family and go home."

Mary reached forward and gently touched his shoulder. "I know. I don't want to be here either. But honestly, after the story you just told, I'm not sure you should be in such a hurry to leave, or to find your... wife. This may be the perfect place to lay low for a while, right?"

Brad clenched his eyes shut and curled fists at his side. He forced himself to breathe as the pressure built in his chest.

Monster

This was not the revelation he bargained for. She was purposely avoiding what he wanted to know.

"Listen," Mary gently began to caress his shoulder. "My offer still stands. Come back to my room and let me take care of you. You look like you could use some stress relief. No one has to know."

That was the final crack in the dam. The building pressure in his chest burst like an escaping xenomorph. He stood up shouting.

"No one has to know! That's the whole problem! That's what started all the trouble in the first place! I never told Sarah how I felt, about her, about being a father! She didn't need to know! She didn't need to know about Valerie - but see how that turned out! You didn't need to know that she fucking killed her and that I helped! Now you want me to do it all over again! You want me to betray my wife, my family? And no one needs to know! You say *I'm* crazy!"

Mary held her hands in front of her. She patted the air motioning him to calm down. She shushed him. Her eyes darted from side to side.

Brad immediately understood her reaction. It wasn't his outburst that concerned her, but what it would attract. He shut his mouth, but the garden had already taken notice. He heard the strange ratcheting noise, rapid clicking like cracking knuckles. He looked out over the garden and saw the waist-high hedgerows begin to rattle and shake. He saw movement like wakes on water converging toward them. Hints of insect limbs broke the surface long enough to reveal their bizarre hard jointed shells.

"Don't move!" Mary said to him. "Stay completely still and quiet and they won't hurt you. They're just panicked. Just don't move." She stood like a statue.

But Brad ran instead.

He took off down the path that headed toward the Sanitarium. Only a few hundred feet lay between him and the outer walls, but there was no telling how many bends the garden path would take to cover the distance.

Then he heard Mary scream.

He turned and looked back. As he watched, the first awful Gardener leaped over a hedge and landed right beside her. It swept one of its many sharp fin-like limbs and took off her arm just below her elbow. She screamed again. A second enormous insect leaped into the circle. It raised itself up on a series of angled legs. Their hard bodies popped and snapped as they rained down their heavy limbs on Mary. She dropped out of view below their onslaught. Their sharp, barbed appendages jabbed and raked, rising covered in blood and shreds of clothing and flesh.

Brad turned away from the slaughter. As he had done before, he dove low to hide himself and used all four of his limbs to race down the path. The building grew nearer with each turn he chose. His hands and feet slapped the flagstone beneath him. His panicked breath filled his ears. But the strange, sick popping and snapping sounds of the horrific insects' limbs grew louder. He could only hope that their own bizarre noises would help to disguise his escape.

The hedges rattled around him. He could feel their presence. They were searching for any threat to the peace of their garden. They were both gardeners and guardians, and he was the invader, the disrupter. Brad had no doubt of his fate if they discovered him. Mary had made that clear.

She knew how to co-exist in their realm. She knew to respect it. And of course, Brad made a ruin of that too. How many would have to die to appease his search for answers? Even now, as he sprang away, he could feel the grip of guilt for his actions, for his own mere existence. But he had to get through this. He still had something to do, a responsibility to uphold. It was all he had left. Perhaps it was all he ever had.

Then he saw the opening. The hedge-lined path broke onto the lawn just ahead.

The Gardeners were all about him, the hedges rattled, he could hear their popping limbs, the scraping of sharp claws on stone. He threw himself forward and rolled out over the grass. The bushes rustled violently behind him, but he did not see his pursuers break through. Slowly the sway of foliage began to calm, and like a strong wind subsided. He saw a single limb, a hard, jointed insect appendage with its barbed fin-like claw. It rose and turned away and sank back into the hedgerows.

Brad dropped flat on his back. He needed a moment to catch his breath and to let the tension drain from his body. He needed to gather his wits. Hardening his will, he refused to mourn for Mary. He forced the thought away. Like Ray before her, he doubted anyone would care or even remember that she existed. She was a contradiction as much as this place was. She'd tried to tell him that this place was just a hospital and that he was as crazy as the rest of the residents. All the while accepting that hideous cave crickets the size of lions roamed the gardens at night. She hadn't even tried to reconcile those realities. The fact that they had just ripped her body to shreds was proof positive to Brad that he was part of something beyond the reality he knew. This was not just a hospital. She had lied to him. He half expected to look above him and see the shadow of the Leviathan pass over and to feel its crushing presence. But there was nothing, only the lonely alien sky.

Something had changed though; despite everything he'd seen. He was more convinced than ever that he was not insane. He had seen Sarah with his own eyes. She was here somewhere. But for how long? Some kind of ceremony was going to take place and he had to act quickly. And knowing Sarah was here meant that his son, Jason, was here too. These were the realities that he chose to accept, and so long as he did, he had a goal. He must find them. He got to his feet and headed toward the front entrance.

When he came to the outer foyer, he walked up the steps beneath the balanced arch and the seeing eye and entered the lobby.

Sister Kayla's desk was the beacon of light that made vision possible in the darkness. Once again, she was absent. Brad stepped up to the desk. Nothing had changed, the sign-in book remained entry-free. He dared not pick up the phone this time. He opened the desk drawer and saw the small flashlight roll into view. It was the same one he had abandoned in the playroom with Antony's son. Brad picked it up and slipped it back into his pocket. Among the other objects in the drawer were a set of keys. He'd seen them before, but now he realized how useful they might be. This time, he took the keys and slid them into his pocket as well.

Brad looked down toward the long corridor that left the lobby. He could see only its dim opening in the darkness. He wondered where it might lead him if he chose that path again. Then he noticed something new. The wall behind Sister

Monster

Kayla's desk ran uninterrupted to the far end of the room. At least it always had. But now there was a new opening. Brad closed the desk drawer and walked toward it.

A new corridor led away from the lobby. He was positive this was not here before, but he had come to accept the surreal and changing nature of this place. Hung on the wall at the threshold was a simple marker that read, "Chapel"; an arrow pointed off into the dark. Brad could think of no better place to look for Sarah. She was a believer. After what had happened in the woods with Valerie, it made sense that she would seek prayer and forgiveness in a sanctuary of God. And what better place might there be for a ceremony to take place? Brad stepped into the passage.

The corridor was short. It ended at a set of wooden double doors standing slightly ajar. Flickering light spilled out in a sharp line across the shiny, polished floor of the hall. Brad heard movement and faint voices within. He hardened his will as he approached. Peering inside he saw that there was a narrow foyer. A long sideboard stood against a stone wall across from the doors. Many candles burned there flickering. Brad carefully squeezed inside. There were two arches leading from the entry area. One faced into the Chapel, glowing brightly with firelight, the other contained a spiral stair. Brad assumed it rose to a balcony above.

He peeked into the glowing Chapel. It was as large as a community church. A high arched ceiling, long wooden pews, a tabernacle and alter at the far end. It was lit entirely by candelabras set around the open nave. Brad was struck with an odd sense of de-je-vu as he looked inside. It seemed inspired by memories of places he could not remember being.

The source of the voices he'd heard was obvious. There were people inside. They stood near the candle strewn alter, their backs turned. Four of them wore black hooded robes, another was cloaked in white. One of the figures was speaking. Brad leaned forward trying to hear what was being said when something touched his shoulder.

His heart jumped, and he spun round to see Antony standing behind him. Antony's right eye was purple and swollen, his nose slightly bent, a nostril rimmed with dry blood. He held a finger over his lips and waved for Brad to follow. Then he sprang across the opening and up the spiral stair. Brad struggled with the choice for a moment then followed him.

The balcony was two pews deep and divided by a stone tower that rose from below and continued through the roof. Brad could see the bell-rope hanging down from above. Crouching low, he and Antony crept to the balcony's edge. A solid wooden rail kept he and Antony concealed as they peered down into the chapel.

The figures below stood in order, with the speaker facing huge stained-glass windows on the wall above them. His arms were uplifted as he spoke in a language that sounded like gibberish to Brad's ears. The three other black figures stood behind, completing a diamond formation with the white robed figure kneeling prone in the center. The stained-glass shined down from above. It radiated with light. The colors caught Brad's attention. His eyes grew wide, and his jaw went slack as he recognized the images in the cut glass.

At one side, men on a boat were pictured, throwing another man to the sea. Storm clouds raged over head. Next, a gigantic whale, a great gray beast with a ribbed underbelly, rose and swallowed the man whom they'd set adrift. Finally, this man was alive and praying within the dark belly of the beast.

Brad knew this story. He could only guess that his grandmother had told it to him long ago. It lodged in his subconscious as a child and laid buried in his psyche ever since. Now the tale came back to him with new formed clarity. He understood that a man named Jonah had been cast to the sea, sacrificed to save the souls of his comrades. But never had this sacrifice seemed so unjustified and involuntary.

This story had new meaning now. Brad had glimpsed with his own eyes the creature that the whale represented. It was the Leviathan. He understood that this monster who had been haunting him was timeless. It had even crept into the religion of his wife and of countless millions of others. Surely it had inspired many more tales through the ages. But the idea of it swallowing a single man insulted its potential. The Leviathan of his experience was a swallower of worlds.

The speaker now turned and faced his companions. He lowered his hood. It was Father Gabraulti. The other black clad figures removed their hoods. Sister Monica stood in the rear, flanked by two other nuns. Gabraulti began again in English.

"The joyous time has come," Gabraulti said aloud. "A time to open the doors to the eternal realm. Are we prepared to do what must be done?"

"We are," responded the holy sisters. They bowed their heads.

"Then let us question the traveler," Gabraulti continued.

The three nuns moved toward the figure in white, but their gait was bizarre. All three moved as Brad had seen Sister Monica move before. They seemed to float over the ground trailing their black robes. For the first time Brad thought he saw something move beneath Sister Monica's long habit, something that was not her legs.

Brad had no doubt that the figure in white was Sarah. The two women beside her lifted her to her feet. Sister Monica reached forward and removed the white robe and hood from her shoulders and let it fall to the ground. Even with her back to him, Brad recognized Sarah standing at the center of this bizarre ceremony. She was completely naked, but she stood proud and unashamed. Her skin seemed to glow, and her hair shimmered in the light of the surrounding candelabras and the stained-glass above.

"You stand before us as you were born," said Gabraulti. "Do you accept your emancipation?"

"I do," Sarah answered.

"Do you carry the sins of your life?" he asked.

"I do."

"And what do you ask?"

"To be forgiven."

"What promise do you give in exchange for forgiveness?"

"I promise to leave all behind, to abandon all allegiance, to be a vessel of one mind, to worship in peace and joy, in life everlasting."

"Then it shall be yours," Gabraulti finished.

He looked around at the Sisters and nodded to them. "Let us then together open the doors."

They each closed their eyes and lifted their faces. Gabraulti stood watching as the Sisters removed their head coverings.

Brad cringed as he saw their forms begin to change. He wondered if his eyes deceived him as first their skin tones grew paler. Then their hair began to fall from their scalps as if pushed out from within. Their bodies began to twist grotesquely, writhing and growing. Their clothing tore into shreds. Wincing, Brad saw their flesh begin to slough like snakes. They grew taller and wider as their bone structures changed and reformed. What remained of their robes dropped to the floor and their naked bodies took on reptilian form. They had no legs, only thick tails coiled beneath them. Their skin was now sickly pale and translucent, bright blue veins pulsed just beneath the surface. Finally, their backs split open and strange new appendages sprang out and grew, unfolding wet and impotent, like the wings of baby birds just emerged from their shells, too small for flight, but as large as human limbs. To Brad's novice imagination these creatures were the embodiment of the demonic.

All through this metamorphosis, Sarah stood unmoving between them. She did not flinch. "I'm ready!" she said in a loud strong voice. She seemed proud and unafraid.

The strange gargoyles, their transformations now complete, stood sentinel around her. They stretched out their powerful arms, touching their claws to each other, creating a circle surrounding Sarah. They chanted in unison in voices that were no longer human. The sound was screeching but soulful at once. It grew louder and louder. Brad had to cover his ears. The entire chapel began to strobe in and out of existence. He saw Ray standing in Gabraulti's spot, presiding over piles of poisoned corpses, he saw the ruined chapel where Antony had sacrificed his only son. Brad cowered, remembering the Leviathan sailing through tornadic clouds. Then he was back in the balcony watching this ceremony. His heart pounded with adrenaline. He felt its sting in every pore.

The glow of Sarah's body intensified. She grew brighter and brighter until Brad had to shade his eyes with his hand. The heat singed from far away. Then she burst suddenly into flame. She arched her back and turned her face upward, but she did not react with pain as her flesh began to burn and her hair melted in the flash of infernal fire. Brad expected her to suddenly disappear in some supernatural whirlwind. Instead, her body blackened and roasted until it finally lost integrity and collapsed in a bright smoky heap among the circle. It lay scorched, burning, and lifeless between the ring of gargoyles.

Brad started to get up. He wanted to curse and shout down at the demons responsible for burning his Sarah alive, but Antony grabbed him from behind. Antony clamped his hand over Brad's mouth and pulled him down behind the balcony rail. Brad found he could not fight back. His body betrayed his efforts to struggle.

"It's too late for her," Antony whispered into Brad's ear. He held him tightly in his lap from behind. "But we can still try and save your son."

Chapter Thirteen

Antony managed to get Brad out of the chapel without being accosted by the strange creatures within. He practically dragged him through the dark hallway to the lobby. Once they were through the doors which led up to the second floor, he sat Brad down on the steps. Antony was sweating and out of breath from half carrying his companion across the building.

"Come on, Brad," he said in a quiet voice. "We need to get out of sight. They'll be coming soon. We can't let them find us down here. Who knows what they'll do?"

"Who cares," Brad answered. His posture was limp as he leaned back against the steps. "They've killed my Sarah. I finally found her and now she's gone. I failed. It's all my fault, and now she's dead. I might as well just give up."

"You still have your son to think about," Antony reminded him. "We can still find him. It might not be too late."

"What are we supposed to do? What were those things? They were huge…hideous. How can we fight against that? They have some kind of powers over the mind. I don't know. I can't believe what I've been seeing, but it's real, isn't it? It's real."

"Yeah, it's real," Antony said.

"They have something to do with that thing, the Leviathan. They follow it, worship it. I saw the pictures in the stained glass. It's like right out of a fucking bible story. But it's more than that. You know what I mean. It made you do what you did, didn't it? It made Ray kill those people in his church too. It's the monster of all monsters. It has me trapped here. It caused the flood and took my family away. And it wants me too. It wants to destroy everything about me. We can't hide from that."

"We might not have too," said Antony. "That thing might be everywhere and see everything, but that may be a weakness. It can't focus on everything at once. If we keep our heads, if we can stay low, then maybe it won't notice us. We have to be like mice in the walls. It may know we're here, but maybe it won't bother to do anything about us. At least not right away."

"What makes you think that? What makes you think it won't notice or care?"

"Because if it does, then we're all screwed," Antony said. "Besides, what choice do we have? We can either give up, or we can look for your son. Maybe we can help him in a way that I couldn't help mine. Maybe that's all we can hope for. A chance to do what's right."

Brad sat up and wiped tears from his eyes. "You're right," he said. "Jason's still here somewhere."

He took a moment to pull himself together. Sarah was gone. He had to burn that reality into his brain. He had to accept it. He refused to admit that a part of him was relieved.

She was one less responsibility to gnaw at him. One more piece in this horrible puzzle-game that had been removed from the board. He hated himself for that sense of relief. He wanted so desperately to be a good man, a good husband and father. But once again he had proven himself a miserable failure. Only one more chance remained, saving his son. He looked at Antony and understood the terrible power that had made him kill his own son. "I'm sorry about before," he said. "I shouldn't have hit you like I did. I was wrong."

"It's okay," Antony answered. "I deserved it. I can't turn back the clock. I can't change what happened. I'm damned. I'll never be free from what I've done. But you still have a chance. If I can help you, it may be the only redemption I'll ever know."

"I understand," Brad said. "Thank you." He gazed up the stairway. "You know where we're going, right?"

"Yes," Antony replied.

Brad slowly got to his feet and the two of them headed up the stairs together.

In the upper hallway, a few of the fluorescent lights buzzed and flickered. It made it impossible for Brad's eyes to fully adjust. He and Antony scurried together over the polished green floor. Neither of them spoke a word, but they were together in their destination. They were heading steadily toward the doors of the West Wing.

Brad knew the answers he was looking for must be hidden behind those doors. But they filled his mind with a physical dread that made his stomach churn. He'd been told from the beginning that the West Wing was home to the most dangerous residents of St. Lucius. Now, after all he'd seen, Brad couldn't imagine anything more dangerous than what he'd already experienced. If what lay beyond those doors were worse, then he doubted whether his mind could survive. There was no longer an instinct of fight or flight; now it was fight or die. He knew he had nothing so virtuous as bravery to drive him. It was defeatism instead. Better to face his doom, then to continue in misery. The only way to end this nightmare was to confront it and accept the consequence.

They came to the doors and stopped. This dead end in the hallway was made from the same stone blocks that Brad had seen throughout his time here. He recognized now that this was a place where separate realities came into contact. The oaken doors were large - thick. Brad could smell the ancient planks of wood. They were held together with heavy iron bands and rivets. A black iron plate held a keyhole that sealed them shut.

Brad reached forward and tested the doors. They were locked. Then he remembered the keys he had taken from Sister Kayla's desk.

Before he could retrieve them, he heard a ruckus from the opposite end of the hallway. He heard doors thrown open and the sound tightened his chest. Something was coming. A swift, smooth dragging sound followed. It reminded Brad of the sound of Valerie's body, wrapped in plastic, being dragged into her final grave. He and Antony turned to face the hallway behind them.

Shadows swayed from around a corner in the corridor. They grew larger. Then their source slid into view. Racing forward were the creatures from the Chapel. The winged albino serpents slithered heavy on their thick tails. Their horrible features came in and out of focus as they passed beneath the lights above them, even so, they seemed to radiate a rancid glow of their own. Brad pressed his back against the doors. His legs began to shake.

These things, who had presided over the destruction of his wife, were made even more terrible by the knowledge that they were once priest and nuns, symbols of what was holy, and their lies gave greater dimension to their threat. These were the creatures that had taken him in and deceived him with shelter and kindness. Now he believed it was all a hidden deceit. They were readying him for something else, something sinister. Perhaps a sacrifice for their god, the Leviathan. Now that they were unmasked, they were coming for him. Their treacherous plan would be revealed. Suddenly, whatever horror that lived beyond the wooden doors seemed preferable to confronting the approach of these demons. But was there time?

Antony turned to him. Brad could see a determination on his friend's face.

"Go!" Antony glowered with gritted teeth and flared nostrils. "Find your son! It's time for me to pay for my sins!"

"No!" Brad shouted, but it was too late. Antony sprang away, running toward the approaching creatures. Brad saw no reflection of Antony in the polished floor.

Brad reached into his pocket and pulled out the keys he had removed from Sister Kayla's desk. When he found them in the drawer, they were an ordinary set on a simple aluminum ring. But as they emerged from his pocket, they became a single iron key. It's size and heavy shaft reminded Brad of a key to some dark ancient dungeon. Through some strange magic, it became exactly what he expected he'd need to open doors like these, but there was no time to question.

Brad inserted the key and turned it. He could feel the resistance of the heavy apparatus within, just as he could hear the slithering of the serpent's approach. Wheels turned, and levers raised. He heard Antony's quick footfalls and a shout of defiance, then a grunt and a surreal hiss and crash. Brad felt something slide within the mechanism. With a click the lock disengaged. Brad could not look back to see the fate of his friend. The sound of their commotion drew too close. Desperately pushing one of the doors open, he leaped through and slammed it shut behind him.

Brad pressed his back against the door. A heavy iron latch within the mechanism turned and reset the lock with a solid click. Brad did not feel the door move with the force of the creatures ramming the other side. He felt no resistance at all. Everything around him was still and absolute quiet.

A long corridor stretched out before him, and it was unlike any place he'd seen at St. Lucius. A perfectly square passage, white walls, floor, and ceiling. There were no reflections here. No pictures or windows or doors broke the conformity. There was no source of light, but there was light everywhere, a clean brightness that felt oddly cold and unnatural. Brad's presence here was the only thing that seemed out of place. But he'd left all reasonable choices behind him, assuming there were any left to be made. He stood up straight and began walking down the corridor.

His sense of time and distance was dulled by the lack of reference points. There were no turns or intersecting hallways. He looked behind and saw that the doors that brought him here were gone, only the long endless hallway reaching forward and behind. He began to think of this as a new realm of torture. He'd just escaped a world of darkness, shadow, and reflection, only now to enter a place of light and eternal emptiness, void of sensation and earthly pain and pleasure. If he did not discover something soon, then his mind would surely begin to feed back on itself and devour what remained of his sanity.

With that thought in mind, something did appear, a small round face floating disembodied in front of him. He stopped with a gasp. It was the soft, innocent face of Sister Kayla. He saw now that she was not merely a face. Her habit covered her entire form. It was all white and flawlessly blended with the environment around her. Even her small hands were tucked into her sleeves contributing to the mirage. She smiled at him.

"Hello, Mr. Turner."

Brad was torn in two. On one hand, he knew that she was one of the staff; she was part of whatever demonic Order reigned here. He had seen her colleagues' true form and had to guess that she was also a hideous creature beneath her holy vestments and human appearance. But he also saw the young woman who'd helped him. He'd felt her kindness and her compassion. She'd tried to assist and comfort him with a sense of genuine humanity, unlike the other members of this bizarre and ambiguous cast of characters. At this moment he needed a friend and an ally. But he was prepared for something much worse.

"Sister," he pled. "Please tell me you're not here to destroy me. You're not going to send me to be burned alive and tormented in Hell. If you are, then make it quick. Do it now."

She looked at him with the same smile she'd shown him all along. Her eyes were wide pools of blue.

"Oh no, Mr. Turner, I'd do no such thing. I've come to greet you. You have my key. I've been expecting you."

Brad felt his defiance melting away. "I'm sorry. I did take the keys from your desk. And I took the flashlight back too."

She continued to smile. "Don't worry, Mr. Turner. It's of no consequence."

"Sister," he began with some hesitation. "If you're not here to hurt me, then can you help me? Please, I'm trying to find my son. I'm so lost. Can you please help me?"

"Yes, I know why you're here. Though, you really shouldn't be. It's highly irregular," she paused. "You see, I am the Gatekeeper here. I open doors, and I seal them. The doors you just passed through should have remained closed to you. But… you've captured my sympathy, Mr. Turner. You're a very unusual man." She stopped and looked about, though obviously they were alone. "It seems there has been some mistake," she whispered. "And mistakes are very rare. It's all very curious to me. That's why I've allowed the rules to bend. What is it they say? *Curious times call for curious measures.* For the first time in many long years, I can't see how this is all going to end. Honestly, there is only so much even I can do."

"What is this place?" Brad asked peering around at the dull uniformity. "It's so different from everything else I've seen."

"This is the Repository for lost souls."

"That's what Gabraulti called it, *a repository for lost souls.* What does that mean? I don't understand. Does that mean me, and the others I've seen here? Ray and Mary and Antony, are we the lost souls? Is this a prison where we're supposed to wait for our sentences to be carried out? Or is it just a place to be tortured? Is this our punishment?"

"No Mr. Turner, this is not a prison. Not for you. You have been free to leave from the moment you arrived. But you have to make your own choice about your destination."

"What, like I can just click my slippers together and magically I'm home?"

Sister Kayla smiled broadly. "Believe it or not, I understand that reference," she almost giggled. "But no, things are not so simple. I sympathize with you. You have a rare choice."

"You keep saying I have a choice, but no one will tell me the options. How can that be fair!" he protested. "How can you expect me to make any choice when I don't know what's at stake?"

She furrowed her brow and looked away from him.

Brad sensed that she was struggling. Of all the so-called clergy he had met here, she was the only one who seemed to possess a genuine sense of compassion. But he could tell she was strong willed. He watched her weave her fingers together as she had some internal debate.

"Okay then," he too tried to muster some strength of will. "Then I choose to be with my son. If you say I'm free to choose, then that's my choice. No more word games. I want to see my son!"

"Normally that would be impossible," Kayla said. "But this is a strange circumstance, unprecedented... I'll let you see him, but I warn you. I don't believe it will help. Once you taste of this knowledge, you may be forever tainted. There's no turning back and no way to change what has already come to pass."

Brad looked at her tensely, his mouth went suddenly dry. But he could not abandon his search. He believed that this was no trick or deception.

"Good," he said. "I have to do this. I've come this far. I've already lost my Sarah. I can't bear that I've let them down, that I've failed them so miserably. I couldn't live knowing that I just turned away. I have to follow through. I have to know. Please, take me to my son."

"Very well," she said. "We're already here. Just place your hand on the wall beside you."

Brad felt the familiar rush of adrenaline stream through his veins. Pressure gripped his chest. He didn't know what he had expected, but it wasn't this. His mind grappled with whether he was truly ready for whatever revelation he was about to receive. Maybe he really didn't want to know.

He raised his hand, palm facing out, held it inches from the wall. He was afraid to touch it as if he might be burned. He forced his eyes to remain open. Then he took the plunge and placed his palm on the smooth white wall.

The surface beneath his hand remained solid, but it immediately changed from white to transparent. He was looking into a plain white room. It was square, perhaps ten feet per side. No doors or windows or furnishings of any kind. The only thing within the room was his son, Jason. The boy floated, completely weightless in the center of the square. He was naked and unmoving, perhaps asleep. The child turned in a slow flowing rotation.

Instinctively, Brad pressed himself against the wall. His son was there, just a few feet away, just beyond this impenetrable barrier. Brad could hear no crying or screaming from the child. The boy seemed at peace. And he was alive.

His skin was plump and pink, and his tiny fingers twitched naturally along with small fluid motions of his arms and legs. Brad once again scanned the room for any sign that he might be able to enter and take his son. Then Jason swung in his rotation so that Brad could see his tender face.

Brad blinked to clear his vision, struggling to reconcile what he saw with reality. Jason no longer had eyes. There were no flickering lids covering the optic orbs, only skin that stretched from his faint eyebrows to his high cheekbones. Then Brad noticed that Jason's ears were the same. The ears themselves remained in place, but there were no holes for sound to enter. There were no nostrils beneath his nose. Only his mouth remained. It rested partially open as his small chest rose and fell with breath. Brad moaned, his eyes shot wide, his mouth pulled away from his grinding teeth.

"What have they done?" Brad cried out. "What have they done to my son? His face! Oh my God, his face!"

Brad's knees gave out and he collapsed to the floor. He slid down the clear wall. Like a spear skewered straight through his heart he felt part of himself die. He wailed and cried. Tears burst from his eyes and his nose began to gush. He turned and looked up at Sister Kayla standing beside him. Her face mirrored his pain.

"What have you done to my son?" he pleaded.

"I'm so sorry," she said to him. "No parent should ever see their child this way."

"But why?" he continued to beg. "Why my child? How could anyone do this to a child?"

"He is one of the lost souls," she said. "Too innocent for damnation, but not cognizant enough to choose the worship of our God. They have not been anointed. They have not been baptized. They wait in this purgatory for a time beyond knowledge. It is here that they are cared for."

"Too innocent for damnation?" Brad shouted. "This isn't damnation? If it's not, then I don't understand what that is. Look at this place, there is nothing here!"

"This is far from damnation, Mr. Turner. There is no suffering here. The children feel no pain, they do not struggle or want. They will never know guilt or responsibility, or the loss that you feel right now. They are only forbidden their connection and understanding of the great creation. They do not sense the beauty of the world and its many riches, but they do not sense its troubles or its sufferings either. Their souls are blank vessels waiting to be filled. It is the purpose of this place to sustain them until their time comes… You see, look, it's time for your child to drink of everlasting life."

Brad turned again to the white chamber. Something materialized from the ether behind his son. Brad jerked and stepped back. It was one of the gargoyles. Its albino skin seemed sickly off-color next to the pure white of its surroundings. There was no way of knowing if he'd seen this individual creature before, as its hideous features were uniformly horrible. It stood large on its coiled body, naked and sexless, but for huge, bloated breasts that hung from its vein strewn chest. It reached out its powerful arms and grasped the boy. It drew him in and attached Jason's mouth to one of its long pink nipples. Jason immediately began to suckle greedily.

Brad immediately felt a surge of bile rise into his burning throat. He gagged, but there was nothing in his stomach to purge. He attacked the transparent wall, hoping it was glass that he could shatter with force. It was unyielding. There was neither a reaction from Jason nor the reptilian wet-nurse that fed him its unnatural nutrient. They seemed unaware of any sound or image from outside the cubic cage.

Brad raged. He turned away, unable to look. He threw himself at the corridor wall opposite his son. Immediately that wall became transparent, and he could see through to another white chamber. Inside was another child, close in age to Jason. It too was blinded and senseless, being nursed by one of the nightmare creatures. Repulsed, he moved away, dragging his shoulder against the wall. Another section revealed a new identical chamber and occupants. He touched yet another section with the same result. Brad knew now that the entire corridor, stretching endlessly in both directions, was a prison for these children. An epic warehouse of souls lost in purgatory. The scale he imagined stretched through time immortal. And he realized that any mind that could conceive of such a reality was surely warped and evil beyond comprehension. No other confinement could be so cruel.

Sister Kayla approached down the corridor. She reached a hand toward him.

"Mr. Turner let me help you," she said. "Let me take you away from here."

He backed away. "Stay away from me," he said holding his hands out in defense. "This is evil and you're a part of it. How…how can you live with this?"

"I'm so sorry, Mr. Turner. I knew how this would affect you, but you needed so badly to know the truth. It is the way of the faithful. But I understand how bitter the sight of seeing it with your own eyes. I would have spared you this. Only these poor lost souls know the true bliss of ignorance." She stepped closer still. "Please, come with me. I'll take you away from here."

"Don't you touch me!" he snapped. "Stand back!"

Sister Kayla was small compared to Brad. In her pure white habit, she looked even smaller. Her kind demeanor would not have frightened the tiniest creature. But Brad knew now what she was. She too was a frightful demon. How could he not see her in that light? All her kindness and compassion had been a deceit to force down his defenses. He was no longer capable of trust. He knew at his core that she could likely overpower and destroy him with little effort, and part of him welcomed that.

He suddenly realized how horribly alone he was. Sarah and Jason were beyond his help. They were gone. The only thing left was his own survival, and that was nothing more than a fleeting involuntary instinct. Nevertheless, he reacted defensively.

Brad backed away. He had nowhere to run, nothing to use to fight her off. He reached into his pocket and felt only the small flashlight he had taken from Sister Kayla's desk. At the very least, he thought, he could use it to harden his fist. He pulled it out and immediately felt its sudden weight. Just as the set of ordinary keys had transformed into the key to this horrible place, the small flashlight became a short scepter. A heavy iron rod, eighteen inches in length, strange runes were cast along its shaft and a bright clear jewel mounted at its tip. Its end glowed brightly, much like the light it had transformed from.

Brad stifled his own surprise and held it out in front of him. "Stay back!" he said again. "I swear I'll beat you with this thing. I've got nothing to lose!"

Kayla looked at him with a smile that deflated his confidence. He could see that she saw no threat or reason to fear.

"Come Mr. Turner," she said stepping closer. "Time grows short. Let me take you away from here before the others come. Let me help you."

Brad rushed toward her with the scepter held high. He swung it over his shoulder aiming for the top of her head. He would smash her with it if he could.

As the rod came down, Kayla raised her hand and caught it in mid-stroke. It seemed a simple, casual movement. But when it touched her, both she and Brad were connected. That was enough for her to open the gate.

Chapter Fourteen

Once again, Brad was falling through a blackhole in time and space. Sister Kayla had called herself the Gatekeeper and now Brad understood that this monstrous passage was a dimension of travel opened by her. She was master of the key and the scepter that channeled this power, and she'd lent them both to Brad on his journey. He'd held the flashlight when transported to the ruined church where he'd witnessed the terrible sacrifice of Antony's son. He'd held the key to the stark corridor of purgatory. Kayla claimed it was compassion that ruled her actions, but Brad found nothing of compassion in the fate he and his family had suffered. He was tumbling blindly, like a soulless child, not knowing if or when he might stop, or in what dark Hell or Nirvana he might be imprisoned. He held no notion of hope for himself or for those he loved. He was surrendered.

As suddenly as his fall began, he came to a jarring halt. He opened his eyes and recognized sensations around him. He was on his back. The comfort of short, cropped grass lay beneath his arms and neck, its cool smell like an evening in summer. But it was full night. Above him was the strange alien sky he had viewed from the garden. He had the unjustified impression that this was how the sky had appeared in the early universe, long before the expansion had pushed the nebula and galaxies so far away. He imagined a distant future, where all the fires would be expended, snuffed out by time, and the universe would be nothing but a cold empty darkness.

Then he heard the music.

Immediately he recognized the source, but the tune still eluded him. It was the whistled breath of Mal Livengood that soothed Brad's nerves like a mild narcotic. He couldn't help but lay there a moment longer just to absorb its haunting melody. He made no further attempt to recall where he'd heard it in the past. He accepted its gentle meandering as he might accept the sound of air flowing through trees or a stream trickling down tiny waterfalls. After a moment, he shook his head clear of it and raised himself onto his elbows.

Brad was in a familiar place. He was in the apparent heart of the garden. It was here that he had watched Sarah speaking to Mal shortly before her ceremony of fire. At the center of this round glade inside the hedge-maze, stood the tree. It was even more impressive now that he could see it clearly. Its trunk was massive. Its roots grew from the ground in thick sinewy stalks and fibers. They met and twisted like banded serpents, seemingly independent. Together they made up a column eight feet in diameter that rose above the height of the surrounding hedges. From there its fibers became branches that spread in reflection of the roots below forming an umbrella-like canopy thick with broad leaves. Brad could not see how high it grew through the dense foliage, but he imagined it towering upward, layer after layer. Underneath the canopy, Brad could see fruit hanging from the branches. It was round and plump and glowed with a faint purple luminescence. It was this fruit that gave the glade light, along with the sparkle of something like fireflies in the branches above.

On a stone bench, halfway between the tree and where Brad lay, sat Mal Livengood. Sitting quietly with his legs crossed, he whistled his tune with an expression of pure contentment. He seemed patiently waiting for Brad to gather himself.

Brad wondered whether this was a prelude to his own ceremony of self-destruction. He wanted to be angry. He wanted to stand up in protest. He wanted to curse at Mal and at everyone attached to St. Lucius. He wanted some explanation for what had happened to his family. But in the end, there was only disillusion. It tore at his heart and soul as if feeding on the little that was left of him. He was exhausted. The beauty of this place and the trance-like effect of the music left him drained and complacent. Brad rolled over and slowly pushed himself to his feet.

Mal stopped whistling. "I'd ask you how you're feeling," he said. "But I can see it on your face. Come and sit with me. Let's talk."

Brad came over and sat beside Mal. He looked at the ground. His thoughts were of Sarah and Jason.

"I'm sure it's no conciliation, but this is not how things are supposed to happen. It's unusual. You're unusual." Mal said.

"You're right," Brad answered. "It's no conciliation. Sister Kayla said nearly the same thing to me. It doesn't make any more sense now than it did then."

"I understand," Mal replied.

Brad looked at him and released a brief ironic laugh. "I'm so glad that *you* understand. I'm so happy for you."

"I'm sorry," Mal said. "I didn't mean it that way."

"Look, if you're going to kill me, burn me up, strip me of my senses and lock me away, just do it. I've had enough. I'm done with this place."

"Unfortunately, this place isn't done with you."

"Would you please stop saying things like that. I'm sick of all the cryptic bullshit. I've tormented myself enough, I don't need it from you too."

Mal seemed to consider that. He nodded his head. "You're right," he began. "The truth is the only way we're going to get through this." He paused for a moment as if to gather his thoughts, then he began again.

"This place, this garden, is a… waypoint. It's a junction that connects different realities. It is the center. This is the point where it all began, the epicenter of creation itself. All the universe came into being with a thought, and all things grew from this very spot. At least, that's what we've come to believe."

"You see, no one knows whether the universe was of conscious design. Whether the rules that govern it were intentional, or whether the rules were made necessary in light of the nature of reality. But in either case, there are rules, and they are rarely broken."

"This sounds like a bunch of metaphysical mumbo-jumbo to me," Brad interrupted. "What rules are you talking about? Did I break some kind of rule? Are you saying this is my fault?"

"There's a natural order to things," Mal continued. "The necessity of freewill is part of it. Eventually, everyone makes a choice. Most people aren't even aware that they've made one."

"It comes down to this. One chooses to spend eternity in service and worship of the Almighty Creator, or they choose the endless cycle of what you'd think of as Hell, to live over and over again in conflict and strife. But the choice must be freely made. It can't be imposed by another."

"That's why there are so many children caught in Purgatory. In life, they weren't capable of understanding the choice, they were too young for a choice to be tangible. So, they wait, outside and disconnected from God, until a time beyond our knowing." He paused. "I swear to you, I don't know what the future holds for them."

"That's so fucked up," Brad shook his head aghast in the thought. "What kind of God would set rules like that? I don't understand."

Mal looked with sympathy but seemed to have no good response.

Brad continued. "But this choice you're talking about? I didn't make any choice?"

"As I said, not everyone makes the choice consciously. There are those who spend their entire lives professing their love of God, convinced of their place in Heaven, but whose hearts are so filled with corruption that their very pleas for forgiveness betray themselves as lies. They believe they've made one choice, but really, they have only deceived themselves. And then there are those who spend their lives in selfish and evil pursuits. But if they truly repent, then their forgiveness comes with eternal life and salvation."

"Fortunately, those are the exceptions. As you might expect, the good usually wind up in Heaven and the bad in Hell. It's just to say that not all decisions people make are made with self-awareness. Sometimes they are only evident in the true nature of one's spirit."

Brad struggled to comprehend what Mal was saying. He had never believed in any of this. But now he had experienced so many strange things, things that could only be described as supernatural. But what was supernatural? What did that really mean? If it were real, however bizarre it seemed, then it was part of the natural world. He wished he could still cling to the idea that he had lost his mind. But that was cold comfort now.

As he contemplated these new realities, Brad felt a sudden change in the air. It was a feeling more than anything else, an intuition. The hair on the back of his neck stood up. He looked around and saw hedges begin to tussle. His adrenaline spiked.

"They're coming," Brad said lowering his voice. "The Gardeners. They're attracted by noise. They tore poor Mary to shreds. We've got to get out of here."

Mal smiled. "There's no need to be afraid of the Gardeners. They won't harm you here. They only attack when they perceive a threat to the peace of the garden."

"Are you sure? I've seen what they can do, it's horrible. What are they?"

"They're the firstborn. Perhaps as old as the garden itself. No one knows. They were here long before any of us. They're the guardians of all things that grow, plants and trees and all things that root. But it's not the Gardeners you hear. Someone else is coming."

Brad could think of only one thing that was as frightening as the Gardeners. Mal was speaking of the Gargoyles. Brad didn't know who or what Mal was, but he found it hard to believe that they could withstand a confrontation with those creatures. They were disciples of the Leviathan, and nothing could defeat that awful power.

The glade had several entrances, and through them Brad saw the creatures appear. They slithered forward on their thick tails, stopping before entering the hedge-ring. They seemed wary about something, afraid to come closer. Perhaps the glade itself offered protection or maybe the power of the tree held them back. Brad jumped up and stood behind Mal.

The creatures wavered in place like cobras, their cold reptilian eyes focused on Brad and Mal. In the hedge-break closest to Brad, another figure appeared. It was Father Gabraulti, returned to human form. His neon eyes, salt and pepper hair, and the white of his collar, were tainted by the violet glow of the fruited tree.

"We've come for Mr. Turner," Gabraulti said in a tone that was as kind and compassionate as it had ever been.

"But the choice hasn't been made," Mal answered him.

"These are strange times, and rules have been broken," the Father said. "We have decided what choice must be made. We cannot let the anomaly continue. Mr. Turner needs to come with us. It is for us to decide now."

Mal stood up.

Gabraulti and the others shuffled in apparent apprehension.

"Where is Kayla?" Mal asked, his eyes scanning the circle. "Why isn't she with you?"

"You know exactly why she isn't here. She broke the rules."

"And you think that's had no effect? You're trying to cover your ass Gabraulti. It's not like you to be so impulsive."

The Father scrutinized Mal for a moment but did not respond.

"Mr. Turner is under my protection for now," Mal said to him. "You're right, rules have been broken. And if we're to set things right, then I may break some more." Mal stood straight and tall. He did not look like a custodian anymore. "Are you going to stand in our way?" he challenged.

The Father stood considering, keeping his eyes focused on Mal's. Gabraulti remained silent a moment longer, then relented. "As you wish," he said with a slight bow.

He turned and went back into the labyrinth without another word. The Gargoyles surrounding the glade also turned. Silently they too disappeared back into the greater garden.

"Holy shit, Mal! What the hell's going on?" Brad's mind was racing. "What did he mean that these are strange times? And the anomaly? Was he talking about me? Am I the anomaly?"

"You need to understand," Mal answered. "This process has been going on since mankind first appeared. It's been a test of trial and error ever since. None of us really know how any of this works. No one knows the Creator's mind. There may not be any *mind* behind it at all. But somehow, you've managed to avoid making a choice and now you're stuck here, here in the middle of creation."

"I have no doubt that you're a good man," he continued. "You've always tried to do the right thing. You've been driven by ideas of commitment and responsibility. Even when confronted by Sarah's murderous crime, you accepted *her* blame. You're a martyr without the narcissism. But you carry so much guilt. It's like the boulder of Sisyphus. It crushes you and influences everything about you. Every fiber of you craves punishment and damnation, but your soul seems to long for redemption. You're a conundrum, unlike any we've seen, an anomaly, in perfect balance between Heaven and Hell."

Brad didn't like being examined like this. He was red-faced and tense, but he couldn't offer a denial. Then something even more profound entered his thoughts.

"Wait a minute," he interrupted. "With all this craziness I missed the real point. Are you saying I'm dead? All this talk about Heaven and Hell. This is like, *now* we're talking about. I need to make this choice now because I'm dead now. Is that it? Am I dead? Sarah and Jason, are we all dead? Did we drown in the flood?"

Mal blew out a breath and palmed his forehead. "Well, yes and no."

"You mother fucker! That's not an answer! You tell me right now! Are we dead?"

"Yes," he answered. "In the sense that you understand it, I guess you are. I don't know how else to answer you. Things aren't as simple as that. You're in transition. Is that better? You tell me, do you feel dead? Is this what you thought of when you thought of being dead?"

"Of course not!" Brad tried to calm himself. He took a deep breath. The truth was that he didn't feel dead at all, he felt alive as far as he understood the concept.

"I guess I thought that there would be nothing, like when I died it would just be over. It would be like how things felt before I was born. Nothing. I thought it would be nothing, just final - peaceful. I never imagined anything like this."

The realization slapped him across the face, both stinging and sobering. The thought of death had never frightened him before. Of course, he was afraid of *how* he might die, whether it would be drawn out in a wasting illness, or a sudden, tragic, and painful death. But *being* dead seemed like a comfort. When it came, it would eliminate all the worries of the world, his responsibilities would be lifted, and no new struggles would come. A part of him may have looked forward to that end. The revelation that there was an afterlife was shocking. The thought that he would continue, perhaps forever, was terrifying. In a way, it was a reality worse than the death of his imagination.

His mind wandered. "But what happened to Sarah, if she's dead too, did she go to Hell? I saw her burn up in that ceremony. I saw what she did. She killed Valerie. There can't be a worse sin than that. She killed her twice. First, she thought she was dead, then later, she killed her for sure. And she planned it. I know she did. The shovel and tarp were already in the back of the car. We never kept them there. She planned to kill her and to get me to help her dispose of the body. That bitch! I never would have guessed. How could I be so blind? Mal, tell me. Is she in Hell?"

"No," he answered. "She burned her sins away and asked for genuine forgiveness. In her heart she always worshipped the Creator... I can see what you saw in her, though. She had a nice way about her, very up-beat. I personally found that the psychopathy made her more interesting. That's just me though. As far as I can tell, Heaven is filled with redemptive evil. But it's not my place to judge."

"How can you say that?" Brad responded. "You've judged me. You seem to have some pretty strong opinions about me. How do you know what goes on in my head? What are you a mind reader or something?"

"You don't believe that St. Lucius is a real place," Mal replied. "It's just a construct. It's a framework within which your mind can explore the issues that confront it. We've all been observing you since you arrived. Trying to figure out why you haven't moved on. At first, we believed it was your connection with your family. I'm sure that's what Kayla thought when she gave you help. It's why she waylaid Sarah on her journey and let you see her and your son. But you're still here, aren't you?"

"What about everyone else? Antony, his son, Mary, that psycho, Ray? Were they real or did I just make them up?"

"Real enough," he answered. "They were reflections of the things you brought with you. Your trepidations about fatherhood, about lust, your struggle with fidelity, your atheism. These things are all behind you now, and yet, still you're here."

"So, what am I supposed to do? I don't want to go to Heaven or Hell. I just want it to be over. Mal, I don't know who you are. I don't know what you are. But I'm begging you. Please help me. Kill me. Just destroy me. Feed me to the Gardeners, drown me in the pool or rip out my heart. I don't care anymore. I just want it to be over. I can't stand it. Please Mal, if you have any compassion at all, if you have any power, just wipe me out of existence."

Mal did have compassion. Brad could see it in his dark eyes. But he shook his head slowly and frowned. "I'm sorry Mr. Turner. But what you're asking is beyond me. I simply don't have the power to negate existence. The others would make this decision for you, and I think they're wrong. I think that would be a punishment beyond any I could imagine. And I can't abide by that injustice."

Brad looked at him and dropped to his knees. "Who are you?" he pled.

"I'm someone who still believes in freewill," was Mal's answer.

The pain Brad felt was real, the pressure in his chest nearly unbearable. His face ran with tears.

"But I do believe I understand you now," Mal continued. "I do not break rules lightly, and I do it now because it seems like it's the only way. I do feel for you. Take my hand and I'll show you something of the choice you must make."

Brad wiped his face. He was at the end of his rope. There seemed to be no other option but to accept Mal's help. He had no idea what Mal was prepared to show him, but he was certain that it could be no worse than what he had already experienced. Of course, he continually proved himself wrong.

He reached up and took Mal's hand and together they were removed from the garden.

Chapter Fifteen

Brad could only guess that he was now among the stars. It was the same beautiful span of night sky he had seen above the garden. Bright gaseous clouds in every color imaginable held court among a billon billion stars. He felt no acceleration. He felt nothing at all. He could not see his own body, nor could he see Mal beside him still holding his hand. But somehow, he knew that Mal was still with him. Although Brad had no sense of distance on this amazing scale, he could see one curious feature ahead of them. A single white line seemed to bisect the universe. It was bright and unmistakable, as thin as fine thread. Only while looking at it did he have any sensation of movement, and then, he felt himself hurdling toward it at speeds unimaginable. Yet, however closer they approached, the thread of light never changed its appearance or scale. It remained an object of one dimension.

Thinking that he moved his head to change his perspective was a misnomer, since he did not now possess a physical form, but using whatever law of physics ruled this

Monster

reality, he perceived a change. He could see that the line was an infinitesimally thin edge of a vast two-dimensional plane. This plane stretched in every direction, rolling in gentle waves outward forever toward the unknown boundaries of the universe. Mere comprehension of this small aspect of its enormous structure was enough to baffle and overwhelm Brad's tiny ill-equipped mind.

Now he knew that he was approaching it. The white plane did have a surface of physical form. It comprised more and more of his surroundings. The rolling waves of its movement suddenly gave it scale as he realized he was dropping into one of its colossal troughs. The peaks of the waves appeared hundreds of miles high, and he began to lose detail of their edges over the vast distance between them. Even his sense of the waving surface began to fade as he continued to drop.

Soon he began to see details appear below. A strange texture like sandpaper. He drew closer and closer toward the grains. He noticed movement among them. Each grain was stationary, but they seemed to expand and contract in place. The only pattern was chaos. And there was sound also. An incredible confusion of tones like a billion voices mumbling incongruent. Then he recognized form and he knew what these things were that he raced toward. They were an innumerable mass of human beings.

Suddenly, Brad stood among them. He had physical form once again. Beside him stood Mal watching Brad's reaction to this new environment. Brad took it all in.

Everywhere, from right beside him, to the far reaches of the disappearing horizon, were people. Brad looked down on them because they were all prone and kneeling. Through their complete nakedness he could see that they represented all aspects of humanity. By sex, features, and skin tones, he could see that no one was left out of this collection. The commonality that they shared was in their movement. They were all in the act of raising their heads and arms to the starry sky, then bowing until their foreheads touched the ground before them. There was no pattern to be shared. They all seemed to be in their own state of trance, unaware or unconcerned with the others around them. And the sound they made. Each of them seemed to have a mantra of prayer that was their own, spoken without harmony. The volume was so great that as a mass Brad could feel it in trembling waves. He could hear nothing else.

As he gave further examination, he noticed that these people were changed from their prior forms. Although he could tell male and female from their general characteristics, he noticed that these people had no sex organs. The women retained their breasts, but neither male nor female had nipples. Their underbellies were smooth and barren, their backsides had no openings, and their legs and feet seemed to be fused together as if the ability to walk was no longer a necessity. These fused lower limbs were merely flesh and bone hinges allowing for their continual prostration.

Brad was repulsed by the grotesqueness of his surroundings. These poor souls had been stripped of their natural bodies, their human dignity, and apparently their minds. His impression was that he was witness to damnation incarnate. He turned and looked at Mal and saw that he too appeared to share in his disgust.

Mal reached over and touched Brads' shoulder, and suddenly the volume that overwhelmed his hearing reduced to a bearable level. Brad wracked his jaw to balance the pressure in his head.

"Oh my God, Mal. What kind of hell is this?" Brad asked. His body shook with painful nausea and revulsion.

Mal looked at him with a sad smile. "This is no hell," he said. "This is the membrane of Heaven. Realm of the eternal God. The Kingdom of infinite love."

Brad's mind reeled. It couldn't be true. This horrific place held no resemblance to his image of Heaven. Whether one believed in such things or not, nowhere in human history, in storytelling, in collective conscience, was he aware of such a nightmarish conception of Heaven.

Something moved in the corner of his vision. He looked up and saw one of the hideous gargoyles coming toward the nearby surface. It had large mature bat-like wings. They beat at the air slowing its descent. In its arms it cradled a newly transformed woman, on her face was a look of wonder and amazement. The creature set her on an open spot of ground, and she immediately began to pray and bow with a mindless look of elation. The gargoyle glanced over and spied Brad and Mal. It looked with mild interest then turned, beat its wings, and raised back into the sky.

Brad scanned the horizon and saw more of these creatures coming and going, delivering their cargos of once-human fanatics. It appeared there was a constant influx of tantric worshippers.

"So you see the angels of Heaven," Mal said. "The second born. They are the guardians of living beings, escorts to the eternal Kingdom. Their work is never done."

Brad grabbed at his head. His body cramped and shook. "No, no, no... It can't be true. This can't be the way of it. I don't accept it. I can't accept it... No!"

"I brought you here for a reason," said Mal. "I wanted you to have a chance to see the possibilities of your choice. And to hear from someone who has already decided, someone who's word you may trust."

"What are you talking about?" Brad shouted at him. "Who can I possibly trust in a place like this?"

Mal simply turned and pointed to one of the souls praying on the nearby ground.

Brad traced his gesture. There was a woman among the praying throng, and he recognized her at once even as she faced away from him. He had seen her body many times and in her changed form he still knew her. It was Sarah. She was lifting her arms in unison then bowing with her face to the ground in repeating motion. Brad felt the strain of pity seeing her there. He rushed over beside her and knelt, but she did not react to his presence.

It was then that Mal spoke up. "Sarah, someone has come to see you. Talk to him. Let him know your thoughts."

With those words Sarah stopped her bowing and turned her face toward Brad. Her eyes lit up with perfect clarity. Recognition came at once and she beamed with joy.

"Bradley, oh Bradley, you're here. Oh, thank God you're here. I so hoped we could be together." She shifted on her strange, fused legs and threw her arms around him.

Brad cringed at her touch. For the first time he recognized the similarity of her fused body and that of the serpentine tails of the gargoyle angels. But she was warm and real, and the familiarity of her embrace sank in. He returned her hug with tears.

Brad pulled back and held her shoulders, his mind overflowing with emotion. In her face he saw the positivity that was her natural state. He could see her genuine love for him. And he believed with all his heart that this was no deception. As bizarre and unimaginable as all this was, he believed and accepted it all as true. For the first time in his life, Brad was a true believer.

"I'm so sorry," he said. "I tried to save you. I swear I tried. You and Jason. But somehow, I got lost and I've been trying so hard to find you and help you. I've been trapped near the garden and there were so many horrible things. I thought I was losing my mind. Then I found poor Jason. He's caught in a horrible place. I couldn't save him either, I didn't know how. I've failed you both so badly. But now that I've found you, let me take you away from here. Mal can help us. I'll make him. He can break the rules for us. This can't be it. It can't be the Heaven you hoped for. This horrible place, it's a nightmare."

Sarah reached out and stroked the side of his face. Her expression glowed with sympathy. A happy tear formed on the edge of her eye.

"Oh, my poor sweet Bradley," she said. "None of that matters now. All the troubles of the world are behind us. This is Heaven. It's everything that I could ever have hoped for. You'll see, you just need to give yourself to the Lord. He'll provide for everything. There is no need for material things here, no need for food or shelter. There's no war or strife. You'll never have to worry about anything ever again. You can leave all the stress and conflict behind. Here, there's only peace and love."

"But what about poor Jason? How can we go on, knowing that he's trapped in that horrible purgatory forever? How could we ever be happy knowing that?" He looked at her with pleading eyes, hoping that the plight of their only child would shake her loose from this cult-like fanaticism. He saw no change on her face.

"God makes all things beautiful," she said in return. "You'll see once you accept Him in your heart, once you choose to live in worship. That's all he requires. We only need to love Him and worship Him, and He'll grant us everlasting life. This really is Heaven. It's the Kingdom of Eternal Love."

Brad released his hands from her shoulders and sat back on his haunches. He looked around at the millions upon millions of people around them. Surely, many had been here since humankind first encountered their God. Perhaps this realm had existed for much longer than that. He believed what Sarah said, about there being no need or want. But he also recognized the price of exchange in this nirvana. It cost them all their humanity. He was so tired, so drained. He questioned why he resisted this choice. There was comfort in the thought that all his struggles and grief and guilt could be erased forever. But that was the sticking point, wasn't it? It literally meant forever. He might never die, but he would be condemned to live and love forever. He wondered if an infinity of monotonous love would eventually be stripped of any real meaning. The answer seemed frighteningly simple.

He looked back at Sarah's face. He saw Mal standing nearby. Brad realized that if not for whatever power Mal seemed to possess, Sarah would not even know he was there. It was only through Mal that Brad could share these moments with her. With a whim, that connection would be broken, and Brad would lose her again.

Then Brad felt it, that presence that he had come to fear above all other things. And he could see on Sarah's face that she felt it too. It was the coming of the Leviathan.

Brad wondered if it somehow sensed that he was here. Had the breaking of the universal rules drawn it? Would it bend its mind toward him and destroy him, making any choice meaningless? He looked around at the plane of worshippers. As far as he could see, they began to react. They threw themselves to the ground. They shook and convulsed with horrible spasms. They cried out with nonsense, speaking in tongues. Sarah was the only heavenly resident who was protected and somewhat unaffected by its approach.

"He's coming!" she cried with elated joy on her face. "He shows Himself! He is with us! Oh, great God of the universe! Creator of all! Let us love you!"

She looked frantically at Brad. "Join us Bradley, join us in our love for Him! Look and see his beauty!"

Brad was shaking and struggling to retain his senses. The presence was stronger than it had ever been. He felt like this thing were right behind him, reaching out, and its touch would be lightning, an earthquake, an apocalypse. He forced his head to turn, fighting against his instinct to cower. And he saw it.

The Leviathan filled the alien sky. It was his first time seeing it in its entirety and he felt overwhelmed by its size. It was enormous. It seemed very much in form like a whale, and it moved like a giant sea creature slowly swimming through the depths. But due to its size, it must have been moving swiftly as it approached overhead. It was gray in color with a soft, white-ribbed underbelly. Two huge lateral fins, one hundred yards in length, turned like rudders on its sides guiding its shallow swooping course. Behind it dragged a series of squid-like tentacles, longer still than the bulk of its wedge-shaped body. These appendages waved and trailed in its wake like dead serpents dragged through water. As its body dipped and rolled, Brad saw that it had no eyes, only a strange volcanic opening on its back and from that came the blast of its breath.

The sound shook all of Heaven. The plane beneath their feet rattled. Brad could see the pressure wave rushing toward them through the air. The frequency of it was low, deeper than a bottomless chasm, like enormous brass horns echoing in an endless abyss, but it was organic and emotive. There was a kind of sadness that it evoked, deep and painful.

As the wave struck the plane around them, Brad saw that an invisible dome had covered the small area where he knelt with Sarah and Mal. He guessed that somehow Mal was shielding them. But those outside of this protection were not as lucky. The sound wave sent bodies flying like fresh sawdust blown in a storm. It left a clearing on the plane half a mile wide.

Now Brad was exposed with his two companions. They could not blend in with a crowd. There was no way of hiding or disguise. Brad bowed low, not in worship, but in some flimsy hope of self-preservation. The great Leviathan moved overhead throwing its giant shadow and casting a false dusk over the plane. Brad could hear Sarah beside him. She was crying out as loud as she could, trying to draw the attention of her God, professing her unconditional love and devotion. But Brad suddenly realized the futility of her cries.

He had sensed before that this thing had a strange aloofness. There was no sense of intent. No sense of awareness. There was no sense of caring or concern. It showed no interest at all. The only thing Brad sensed was a need for sustenance. Now he saw this thing clearly. This mindless monster, that had been given credit for all existence, had no other desire than to feed. And the nutrient of its desire was the love and worship of others. This plane was its feeding ground. It had no sense of morality. It had created a universe solely for its own self-preservation. It was the embodiment of narcissism. It had no concept of reward or punishment. The plane of Heaven was a vast sea of krill, and the monster need only pass over it to absorb its own want.

Brad stood up as the Leviathan continued its sweep over the field. He was no longer afraid. Having not been prepared by the gargoyles with any ceremony of fire, he could still see the universe with a human mind. As tiny and insignificant as this mind was, it allowed him to make some judgment of where he might fit into this world. This *was* a kingdom of eternal love, but love was the crop that grew here. It was given without return.

He saw that the bodies that had been tossed away by the Leviathan's breath were now crawling their way back to fill the void around him. Like ragdolls they were uninjured by the explosive blast of sound, and like mindless automatons they continued to bow and worship as they pulled their bodies across the plane. Brad saw an endless field of slaves, mindless seeds spawning feed for a single being. For a monstrous creature who created them for no other purpose but to serve it.

He watched as the Leviathan swam over a giant wave of the vast plane and then disappear from view. He heard one last fading blast of its booming, mournful breath. The sound was lost in the resuming choir of worshipping souls.

"Wasn't it beautiful," Sarah said looking up at him. Tears of joy streamed down her face. "It's the most beautiful thing you could ever see. So wonderful…"

Brad turned to Mal beside him. "She won't leave here, will she? Even if I could take her, she would refuse to leave?"

Mal didn't answer. It didn't matter. Brad knew the answer to his question. He knew the answers to many of the questions he'd been asking himself.

"Once the choice is made, it can't be undone, can it?"

Mal shook his head. "It cannot."

"Can you show me, my other choice? Like you've shown me this one?"

"You've seen what the other choice has to offer," said Mal. "Unlike this place, it is full of conflict and stress, a place of continual struggle and torment. You will not find the peace and forgiveness that you'll find here."

"I'm not sure I ever asked for peace or forgiveness," Brad said. "I'm not sure I ever deserved either." He looked down and saw that Sarah had returned to her mindless worship.

"I'm ready Mal. I've made my choice."

Mal reached out and took his hand once again.

Chapter Sixteen

The next leg of his journey seemed almost instantaneous.

It took a moment for his eyes to adjust. He could smell pine cleaner and chlorine. He stood upon his reflection in a dark intersection of hallway with Mal standing at his side. In front of them were a set of doors that led to the basement of St. Lucius. They were metal, and the bottom halves were blackened as if flames had licked out from underneath. Brad found that image appropriate. These doors had always been a source of apprehension, and appearing before them now confirmed why.

"This is it, I suppose," Brad said to his companion. "I guess I should thank you. You've been very kind to me. I probably didn't deserve that."

Mal returned a gentle smile. "There's no need to thank me, Mr. Turner. I'm just the custodian here. I try to keep things clean and in order. Unlike you, I have no choice but to try and set things right. It was important that you were able to make your own choice."

Brad nodded his understanding. "Thanks all the same," he answered. "You've been a friend." He took a deep breath and faced his fate. He fully accepted that there was no turning back from the choice he'd made.

Slowly the doors swung open of their own accord. A familiar passage yawned before him; a stone stairway lit by candlelight spiraling steeply downward. Brad stepped forward, paused for a moment, then began his descent.

In only a moment the doors were left behind. He touched the stone walls beside him and felt their warmth. His throat was dry, and his heart pumped hard in his chest, but he no longer felt the near debilitating pressure that he'd become so used to. He tried as best he could to restrain his imagination from visualizing what lay below, but the more he fought it, the more vivid the images became.

In his mind he saw a vast cavern of smoke and flame. Rivers of lava flowed and poured from high cliffs. Black demonic creatures clung to the walls like spiders. On a parched plain below, thousands upon thousands of wretched souls cried out in torment. Some were in forced labor, breaking stones with hammers, others were stretched on racks or hung from their feet. All of them were plagued by choking sulfur and heat. Devils of all kinds roamed the halls of the damned carrying whips of fire and red-hot irons. And they laughed and rejoiced in their torturous rampage. Brad felt certain that this Hell of his imagination was only a hint of the damnation that lay ahead. It would surely be more horrible than his feeble thoughts could conjure. His only hope was that, like the everlasting love in Heaven that would lose its meaning over time, so too would his painful torment lose its ultimate sting. He had already become numb to his own self-destruction; perhaps even pain could lose its power to inflict.

Even with these horrible images infecting him, he held his course and hardened his will. Soon he began to see light on the curving walls below. He guessed that he was nearing his destination, but he felt no blast of hot air rising from the depths. Instead, he felt air that was fresh and cool, it carried a scent of morning dew. His pace continued unabated. The light became brighter. Soon he reached the bottom of the stair and within sight, up a short corridor, was an arched opening. It was covered with a hinged iron gate, a perfect match for what he had seen leading into the garden. And like those gates, this one was unlatched and pushed open with little effort.

Brad went through and found himself standing in a forest. Turning quickly, he saw that the gate had vanished and only trees stood around him. Low upon the horizon he saw the sun in its rise. Beams of light speared the forest, piercing through the trunks and foliage. A fine morning mist dampened the mossy ground and the scattered piles of stone and bouldered slopes. A small bird shot through branches like an arrow and Brad could hear the song of its companions.

Brad stood carefully watching his surroundings. He had made his choice fully aware of what it meant. He was sure this was some deception. His imaginings of Dante's Hell told of many levels, and surely this was only one of them. What could be more devilish than showing him something of his desire and then ripping it away and destroying it? Damning him to be witness to the destruction of beauty.

Next, he saw movement in the distant trees. It was just a flash, but he was sure there was someone else nearby. Perhaps some Virgil had come to guide him in this new realm of lies. Brad began to hike in its direction. The forest was a tangle of undergrowth and Brad was forced to weave through it as best he could, but the figure leading the chase stayed always just ahead. Brad tripped and fell, muddying his hands and clothes. But he persisted. He was back on his feet, now running faster in his pursuit. He could feel his own exhaustion catching up with him. How long had it been since he'd slept? How much time had passed overall? Had it been days or years? Neither would have surprised him. He did know that he was almost depleted. He would not be able to maintain the hunt much longer.

Finally, he stopped. He leaned forward with his hands on his thighs trying to catch his breath. His lungs stung, and his side cramped. Whoever was ahead of him was going to escape. In a moment he looked up, wiping sweat from his brow with his dirty hand. He stood suddenly straight. Whoever he'd been chasing had stopped as well. They stood unmoving ahead through the trees. Brad could not make out details, but he was sure this was the same figure.

This time, he began slowly. He walked through the trees and around the tangled thorns until he caught up. The figure stood on the brink of a short, steep slope. It stood completely still. One arm was upheld with a finger pointed forward and down the slope. Brad realized at once that this was not a living being, but a statue. It was cast in a grainy, brownish gray color. He wondered if the figure he'd been chasing had continued on, or if somehow it had transformed into the image before him. He stepped up beside it and in a moment of surprise recognized its face. It was Edith, the older woman from St. Lucius. The well-dressed lady who rarely spoke. She was one of the patients who had been in the lounge and in the therapy session. She was the one whom Brad had dubbed, the Witness. It was told that she had seen something so horrible that she was unable to describe it, unable to even speak of it. And now, here was her form, her outstretched arm pointing as guide.

Brad followed her gesture with his eyes. The slope dropped through thick trees. He could see something shimmering in sunlight and he could hear the babble of water. He looked back at the statue. It was amazingly realistic, so much so, that he reached over and touched its face with his finger. Whatever bound it together failed with his touch. The statue lost all integrity and collapsed into a million grains that piled in a heap on the forest floor.

Brad gasped and stepped back. He looked at the grains that remained dusting his fingertip. He rolled them between finger and thumb. He brought it to his tongue. It was salt.

Brad's heart renewed its quickening. This collapsing pillar of bitter salt was confirmation that he was not somehow free from his choice. This was not a forest of good tidings. There was something ahead to be witnessed. Something so horrible that it could corrupt minds and turn beholders to dust. This was a sign of the Hell of his expectation. He locked his jaw and began to shuffle down the slope.

He half-fell, half-slid down the embankment, reaching out and grabbing at saplings and roots to keep his balance on the soft, leafy slope. Finally, he broke through into a thicket of thorny bushes at the bottom. The sharp thorns caught his clothes and scratched his skin with cat-like efficiency. He had to wriggle his body to free himself of their barbed-wire clutches. Large round stones under his feet tried to roll his ankles, but he managed to remain upright. His motion finally stopped, and he was able to look about at his surroundings.

He found himself standing in a wide creek bed. The water was low, and it hugged the high embankment behind him. Across its rocky banks was the grassy floodplain of an oxbow that curved away from him in both directions. The forest climbed less steeply up slopes on the far side. Water at his feet ran steadily over the stone bed. Its sound was cool and soothing. Brad gazed at it for a moment looking for any sign of life - a minnow, a tadpole, even a water bug skipping on its surface. All he saw was a faint, oily, rainbow slick riding along the current. Brad turned upstream and saw a large debris pile where the creek began to make its sweeping turn. Branches and fallen trees were piled high against a series of boulders on the water's edge.

Brad moved against the current, walking in the ankle-deep water. He moved slowly across the slippery rock. As he approached the chaotic debris, he noticed that it was littered with trash and flotsam. There was paper trash, plastic bottles, Styrofoam packaging. He saw a flash of sunlight on chrome. As he edged around the jumbled heap, he stopped wide-eyed and frozen. Balanced against the shattered limbs of ruined trees was a car. It sat tilted on two wheels, its driver's side door facing down toward the water. It was battered and dented. Wet grass and mud jammed its crevices. The windows were filthy and blurred. He could not see inside. This was the wreckage of his own car and it lay dead and derelict.

A burst of adrenaline spurred his sudden action. He bolted forward stumbling over the wet stones beneath him. Brad dropped to his knees and grabbed the handle of the driver's side door. He yanked and pulled at the dented frame, until finally it released. As the door dropped down, so too did the bodies of his wife and child.

Sarah fell into his lap. She was still clutching their child in her arms. They were wet, gray skinned and horribly bloated.

Brad cried out in a moan that was nearly inhuman. He pulled back and away. As he moved, their bodies slid out further. Sarah's legs remained in the car, but her head and back now lay in the shallow water. Her head began to bob back and forth in the current as if slowly expressing her mindless dismay. Jason's tiny hands still clutched in death at his mother's sopping blouse.

Brad's heart pounded painfully. He could feel its hammering in his temples. His teeth ground together as if they might break. A horrible, sickening moan escaped his throat again, low, and wobbling. The inanimate nature of the corpses triggered his gag reflex. But there was no doubt of their identity. This was his family, abandoned and disgraced. Brad forced himself to reach forward. He pulled them completely from the vehicle causing Sarah's legs to shift and turn downstream. He quickly grabbed her from under her arms and dragged her up so that her back rested against his chest.

Brad sat in the creek, leaning against the side of the car and the large rock where it was wedged. His arms wrapped around his dead wife. His fingers weaved together over the body of his baby boy. He was paralyzed by their cold wet touch, their dull lifeless eyes, the blue of their lips and eye sockets. And he wailed at their loss, tormented by his impotence.

It was then that he noticed he was not alone. From the high grass across the creek several people were slowly approaching. They were West Virginia State Police. They came crouched with handguns drawn and focused in Brad's direction, alerted by his moans of agony. They stopped, taking position just on the far bank of the creek, and their faces reflected the horror before them.

"Is that them?" one of the cops asked aloud.

Two young men in camouflaged hunting fatigues stepped out from behind. They both looked nauseous and traumatized by what they were witnessing. One of them spoke up.

"That's the guy. And the woman too. They murdered that girl and buried her in the woods. We saw the whole thing from our hunting blind. That's them alright."

The lead cop took another step forward still training his gun. He looked at Brad with hateful scorn. "You're gonna fry, you son of a bitch. You're gonna fry for what you done."

Brad returned their stares with his own wide eyes and gaping mouth. He began to cry again. His cries turned to demented laughter filled with pain and torturous self-pity.

It was then he heard music; a sad and mournful dirge that further fed his pain and confirmed that he had finally met his destiny.

Clinging to the top of his car he saw a gargoyle perched, but unlike others he'd seen, this one was black as tar. Its skin, burnt and charred by flame. Its lips were the source of the sad melody echoing in his head. Brad understood that no one else could see this apparition, and he understood why. The dark eyes that stared down at him were familiar. They were the eyes of Mal Livengood. He'd come to see that the final pieces were back in place, that things were set right, as they should have been from the beginning. And his demon eyes were the only ones that showed any sign of sympathy.

Monster

Christopher Cunningham

About The Author

Christopher Cunningham received his J.D. from the University of Idaho, Moscow. He is the father of four sons and currently lives with his wife, Annie, and their dog, Gracie, in the mountains of Western Maryland. *Monster* is his debut novel.

Made in the USA
Middletown, DE
24 April 2022